EASY PREY

JOSEPHINE BELL

Josephine Bell had two careers: medicine and writing. After studying at Cambridge, she did further work at University College Hospital, London. She retired from medicine in 1954 to devote all her time to writing. She was described by *London Mystery Magazine* as 'a craftsman of the highest order. Her novels rank among the very best detective fiction.' Josephine Bell's crime novels include *Double Doom* and *Death in Clairvoyance* as well as *The Port of London Murders*, reprinted in the Pandora Women Crime Writers series. She died in 1987.

Already published in Pandora Women Crime Writers:

To be published in 1988:

These will be joined in the future with more novels by Josephine Bell, Ina Bouman, Pamela Branch, Christianna Brand, Celia Fremlin, Gladys Mitchell, Baroness Orczy and many other of the best women crime writers.

EASY PREY

JOSEPHINE BELL

London

First published in 1959
This edition first published in Great Britain in 1988 by
Pandora Press (Routledge)
11 New Fetter Lane, London EC4P 4EE

Set in Linotron Sabon 10/11½pt
by Input Typesetting Ltd, London SW19 8DR
and printed in Great Britain
by Cox & Wyman Ltd, Reading

British Library Cataloging in Publication Data
Bell, Josephine
Easy prey.—(Pandora women crime
writers).
Rn: Doris Bell Ball   I. Title
823'.912 [F]   PR6003.A525

ISBN 0–86358–271–0

Pandora Women Crime Writers

Series Editors: Rosalind Coward and Linda Semple

In introducing the *Pandora Women Crime Writers* series we have two aims: to reprint the best of women crime writers who have disappeared from print and to introduce a new generation of women crime writers to all devotees of the genre. We also hope to seduce new readers to the pleasures of detective fiction.

Women have used the tradition of crime writing inventively since the end of the last century. Indeed, in many periods women have dominated crime writing, as in the so-called Golden Age of detective fiction, usually defined as between the first novel of Agatha Christie and the last of Dorothy L. Sayers. Often the most popular novels of the day, and those thought to be the best in the genre, were written by women. But as in so many areas of women's writing, many of these have been allowed to go out of print. Few people know the names of Josephine Bell, Pamela Branch, Hilda Lawrence, Marion Mainwaring or Anthony Gilbert (whose real name was Lucy Malleson). Their novels are just as good and entertaining as when they were first written.

Women's importance in the field of crime writing is just as important today. P. D. James, Ruth Rendell and Patricia Highsmith have all ensured that crime writing is treated seriously. Not so well known, but equally flourishing is a new branch of feminist crime writing. We plan to introduce many new writers from this area, from England and other countries.

The integration of reprints and the new feminist novels is

sometimes uneasy. Some writers do make snobbish, even racist remarks. However, it is a popular misconception that all earlier novels are always snobbish and racist. Many of our chosen and favourite authors managed to avoid, sometimes deliberately, the prevailing views. Others are more rooted in the ideologies of their time and when their remarks jar, it does serve to remind us that any novel must be understood by reference to the historical context in which it was written.

Linda Semple
Rosalind Coward

CHAPTER 1

Twenty-six Sandfields Avenue, South-West London, was a corner house. Redland Close, a small off-shoot of the avenue, composed of eight houses, cut off number Twenty-six from its neighbour, Twenty-eight, by an appreciable gap. This gave the Holmeses, who lived in Twenty-six, a rather larger, different garden from Twenty-four, huddled against it on the other side. And since Redland Close was not a through road, and not all of its inhabitants had cars, there was hardly any additional traffic nuisance.

Reg Holmes, who was buying the house on a mortgage, was proud of its site. Only number Twenty-eight, of all the sixty-four houses already built on Sandfields Avenue, had a garden of the same shape and size as his own, and even that was a mirror image, and so not identical. Mavis, his wife, was not so sure. A larger garden made more work for Reg, especially at week-ends. Also two boundaries, giving upon roads, and one from the back garden at that, held a future menace to her family. At present, since Joy was only a baby, she did not have to worry. And in any case she admired Reg for his independent point of view, and the energy with which he upheld it. No council house if they could help it, he had decided. And it was certainly paying off now, as they frequently told one another. Because in a council house you could never let rooms, so they would not have found Miss Trubb. The helpful, friendly, motherly, indispensable Miss Trubb.

One autumn evening, when Joy was just over six months old, Reg and Mavis were getting ready to go to a party with

1

friends who lived between Roehampton and Hammersmith.
Reg, who was an engineer draughtsman, in his firm's
designing department, had had a trying day at his works, and
was tired.

'Do we have to dress up?' he asked, wearily, following his
wife into their bedroom.

She had ironed her taffeta dress that afternoon, and set her
hair and done her nails, all in time snatched from the usual
routine. She was not going to be put off.

'Please yourself,' she said, in a slightly irritated voice. 'It's
their third wedding anniversary, and Carol was my best friend
at the office. She's still working there, and her boss said he
might come. Besides,' she added, smiling again as he went
nearer to her, 'I like dressing up. Don't you want me to look
nice?'

He pulled her close and kissed her. They were still very
much in love.

'O.K.,' he said, groaning to stress his sacrifice. 'I'll change.
Not that it makes all that difference. One suit or the other.
Both new when we got married.'

'Don't be silly. You've kept one for best, haven't you?'

'I suppose so.'

They went on dressing in silence, until Mavis said, with a
little sigh of gratitude and satisfaction, 'If it wasn't for Miss
Trubb, we wouldn't be able to go at all.'

'I suppose we could've got someone else to sit in.'

'And paid them for it? Anyway, who? We don't know
many people in this part, not to really know. They talk in
the shops, but how many have asked us in?'

'Do you want them to?'

'Not particularly. But you see what I mean?'

'About baby-sitting?'

'About Miss Trubb. She does it for nothing, and says she
loves it, poor thing.'

'Not so old as all that, or she wouldn't be still working.'

'Probably can't afford not to. She doesn't seem to have any
family.'

'Haven't you asked her?'

'About her family? Well, no. She isn't the gossipy kind, is
she? I haven't liked to say anything personal straight out.'

'Come to think of it, do we know where she does work?'

'Not actually. The city, she says. She gets a bus into Wimbledon, and the District from there. Anyway, what does it matter? She's clean and quiet, and responsible, and she pays her rent, and looks after Joy when we want an evening out. So what more do we want from her?'

'Nothing. We're darned lucky to have her, and it's more than we would in a council house.'

'You needn't keep rubbing it in how wonderful you are. I don't have to be told.'

It was Mavis's turn to put her arms round Reg's neck and kiss his wide determined mouth. Their dressing proceeded slowly.

Miss Trubb's room was at the back of the house, looking over the garden. It was the second largest of the three bedrooms. A small room stood over the hall, next to the larger front room. Miss Trubb's door was opposite that of the bathroom.

There was not much furniture in the room, because the Holmeses had not been able to afford it. But the few pieces were modern, gay and highly-coloured, as were the papered walls. It was an incongruous setting for Miss Trubb, with her grey hair, drab suits and solid, middle-aged figure, but she seemed pleased enough with her surroundings. When Mavis had suggested, soon after her arrival, that she might like to bring in a few bits and pieces of her own, she had merely smiled gently and said she had no furniture. Nor had she many clothes when she arrived, though her wardrobe increased slowly as the months went by.

When Miss Trubb came, in answer to an advertisement in the local Press, Joy had been just a month old. There had not been many other applicants. Or rather, several had called, and some had written, but all had retreated on learning that there was a young baby in the house.

All except Miss Trubb. When she had seen the pram in the hall and Mavis had told her about Joy, her stern, rather lifeless features had glowed with a sudden radiance, an inner happiness that shone in her faded eyes and trembled in her voice. Mavis had been quite surprised. She had expected another refusal more definite than the rest. Instead, Miss

Trubb had taken the room at once, asked to be allowed one peep at the new baby, and moved in the very next day.

On the evening when Mavis and Reg were preparing for their party, Miss Trubb sat in her room, near the window, looking out at the blue dusk and the lights in many as yet uncurtained windows. She had not put on her own light, and the newspaper she had been reading as the light faded was still on her lap. She sat very still. It was a habit acquired over many years of forced tranquility and accepted emptiness.

Presently she got up, drew the curtains and set about making herself a small supper. Though Mavis encouraged her to use the kitchen, she preferred a gas-ring in her room. It was set above the gas fire, and here she boiled a kettle for her tea and poached an egg, or warmed a fishcake or a meat pie and some baked beans. She enjoyed preparing these little meals, and eating them at a low table near the fire, under the light of a table lamp set on the mantelpiece. She ate in a silence unbroken by radio or television, both of which she told Mavis she disliked. Undisturbed too, by books or magazines. She enjoyed her peace, her long-sought and hardly achieved seclusion. She had dug slowly into this burrow of retirement, and now she sat deep in its quiet warm compass, not moving because she had left no room to move, but safe, because the enclosing walls pressed comfortably on every side. Or so she hoped, and tried, in her more energetic, more fearful moments, to persuade herself.

Reg and Mavis stopped outside her door before they left the house, to call out to her that they were off, that Joy was asleep, and that they did not expect to be later than eleven.

Miss Trubb swallowed a mouthful of cake, got up and went to the door, a smile beginning to widen her mouth as she did so.

'I'll be here,' she said, and laughed at her unnecessary statement.

The young parents laughed too, and ran down the stairs, hand in hand.

After they had gone Miss Trubb stood on the landing, her head on one side, listening. The house was very quiet. Noises from the world outside came through the open window on the staircase, but they were distant, impersonal as far as she was concerned. Traffic; children in the gardens, who ought to be in bed, she told herself; some chopping logs for firewood. Busy people, far away, who could not any longer trouble her, or even find her. Inside this silent house she was quite alone, except, of course, for the baby.

She moved along the landing to the small bedroom over the hall. This was Joy's nursery, where she slept by herself, in accordance with modern practice. Miss Trubb thought it a shame, but had never said so. Not for anything would she interfere with other people's beliefs and rules.

She crept softly into the room and stood beside the cot looking down. Joy had snuggled low under her blankets. Only her short fluffy hair showed above them. Miss Trubb put out a finger to stroke the hair.

The baby moved. A bright pink cheek appeared, dewy with sweat. The little nose wrinkled, the mouth twitched. Then with a faint sigh Joy slid back into her deep sleep.

Miss Trubb carefully folded down the blanket. Joy was obviously too hot. It was not good for her. She stood for a few seconds afterwards, the lines of her face softened, but more expressionless than ever. Then she turned and went back towards her own room. But as she was about to move into it the front door bell rang, splintering the silence of the quiet house.

Miss Trubb drew back, lifting her hand to her throat. Bells terrified her, even ordinary electric front door bells. She swallowed twice, fighting her unreasonable fear. By the time the bell rang again, she had mastered it.

'Just tell whoever it is they're out,' she whispered to herself. 'That won't hurt you. They're out. You only have to say that, then they'll go away. Go away,' she repeated to herself, aloud, and began to walk down the stairs.

Reg and Mavis arrived at their friends' house to find pandemonium, with Derek Fry suddenly and mysteriously ill, Carol in tears, and six other guests helplessly flinging advice, and getting in one another's way.

'He was pouring drinks,' Carol managed to tell them in the hall, 'and he sort of fainted. But he was out for ages. At least it seemed ages, and now he's shivering all over, and he says he can't move his legs.'

Reg and Mavis exchanged a quick horrified look, which Carol saw, and which brought on a fresh burst of tears.

'Polio!' she sobbed. 'That's what they're all hinting. I can't bear – '

'How long ago did this happen?' Reg asked, in a sharp, sensible voice that made Carol gulp to control herself.

'Half an hour. People had only just started coming. They kept coming – '

'Look,' said Mavis. 'The party's off, and I'll get every one to go home – *now*. Have you called your doctor?'

'I think so. Roy said he'd do it.'

'I'll check,' Reg said, briefly, and went away to do so.

Mavis was turning away too, but Carol stopped her. 'Don't go,' she begged. 'You and Reg stay on a bit. Till the doctor's been. Derek would feel better with Reg here. It's the others. They keep saying such awful things – about cases they've heard of. . . .'

Mavis comforted her friend and promised to stay. By the time the doctor arrived, order of a kind had been achieved, and hysteria driven out, or at least suppressed. Derek had been carried to his own bed upstairs, the Fry children had been soothed, and were also in bed, probably asleep.

The doctor's verdict was a surprise, but calming. Derek was suffering from an attack of malaria. He had done a spell in the East during his National Service with the army. He had had one mild attack of malaria there, quickly controlled, and had not given it a thought since. The doctor produced an emergency dose, reassured them all, promised to call in the morning, and left. Derek's temperature rose another two degrees.

'Well, what about it?' Reg said, as Carol and Mavis collapsed into armchairs in the sitting-room. The latter sat up.

'Heavens, look at the time!' she said. 'Nearly midnight! Miss Trubb will be wondering where on earth we've got to!'

Carol's white face looked more strained than ever, but she said nothing. Reg saw her distress.

'Would you like us to stay?' he suggested, gently. 'We'd have to go back and fetch Joy. But if you'd like it – '

'Yes, of course,' Mavis agreed, eager to help her friend. 'Or would it be more trouble having us here?'

Carol was overcome, grateful beyond expression.

'You *are* angels!' she kept repeating, and could not find anything else to say.

Reg and Mavis drove home in their little old Austin. They spoke hardly at all on the way. It had been a sad, anxious evening, very different from the gay time they had expected. But at least Derek was not in danger, however uncomfortable, and their momentary panic for themselves and Joy, in a possible polio contact, had proved groundless.

The house was in darkness when they reached it. They went in by the side road, stopping at the garden gate in Redland Close, because their own front gate squeaked. So they could see the back of the house as well as the front, and there was no light anywhere.

'She's gone to bed,' Mavis said, with a faintly indignant note in her voice.

'Do you blame her? She's got to be up and off by eight, poor old girl.'

'But if Joy woke up?'

'Do you stay awake all night on the off chance? I know darned well I don't.'

'No, of course not. But – '

'Well, open the door. You don't want to sit in the car all night, do you?'

Reg found his key, fumbled with the lock, for it was a dark night, and went into the house. Mavis followed. She sniffed loudly.

'Gas!' she exclaimed, in a loud voice.

'Rot!'

'It is! I can smell it!'

They switched on lights and went quickly to the kitchen. Here the smell was obvious and fairly strong, but no taps were turned on, and the wall ventilator was open, though the window was shut. They opened the latter, and went through the other rooms, finding hardly any smell at all. Puzzled, a

7

little anxious, they went upstairs, the faint smell retreating as they mounted.

'She must have been cooking something, and maybe it boiled over and the gas leaked for a minute or two. It smells for ages when you do that,' Mavis suggested.

Reg, who had not taken the gas smell very seriously, was thinking of their immediate plans.

'Better tell her the form,' he said. 'It's a shame to wake her up, all the same.'

'She'll hear, like as not. I'll have to move Joy into the carry-cot, when I've potted her.'

'She'll think that's the usual, if she hears. We'll have to tell her. Can't let her find the house empty in the morning.'

They made their preparations first, packed a bag with their night things, changed into day clothes, put together what they needed for Joy. Then, while Reg was carrying it all out to the car, Mavis knocked gently at Miss Trubb's door, wondering how deeply she slept, how many times she must knock, and if she would have to go in at last and shake her lodger awake.

But none of this was necessary. The response to the first gentle knock came at once, so quickly that afterwards Mavis decided Miss Trubb must have been standing at the time just inside the door.

It opened instantly, wide on the darkness of the room behind. And in the black void was Miss Trubb, moving slowly forward until the landing light fell on her grey hair and stocky figure, and pale set face.

She was fully dressed, and held a pencil in her right hand.

CHAPTER 2

Mavis gulped and took a step backward on the landing, disconcerted rather than alarmed. Miss Trubb stopped at the threshold of her room. Reg, coming back up the stairs, also stopped.

'We didn't want to disturb you,' Mavis began, on the defensive against the unusual. 'We thought you were in bed, as we didn't see a light.'

Miss Trubb stretched a hand behind her to the switch beside the door. Instantly her room sprang into reassuring, coloured, ordinary cosiness, no longer a vague limitless menace. Reg gave a short laugh of relief.

'You must be wondering why we've knocked you up at all,' he began. 'The fact is. . . .'

Miss Trubb listened to the tale of Derek's sudden illness, her calm face turning from one to the other of the storytellers. She did not seem to be surprised or even very much interested, until Mavis said, 'So we promised to stop over with Carol until the doctor's been again. At least I can. Reg has to go off to work tomorrow morning same as usual. So we just came back to change and fetch Joy.'

'Fetch Joy,' repeated Miss Trubb. For the first time her face changed. A flash of relief, or was it disappointment, lit her eyes and trembled at the corners of her mouth. But she only nodded, and said quietly, 'Of course. I'll see the house is locked up when I leave, myself.'

'You *are* good!' Mavis's exclamation was heartfelt and warm, and Miss Trubb's eyes clouded when she heard it, perhaps with tears. Reg, who was watching her closely, was

9

sure of this at the time. Mavis afterwards wondered if she had resented the praise.

They took Joy away in her carry-cot and Carol had a room ready for them. Derek had been off his head, she told them, seeing things and raving, but he had begun to sweat at last, and seemed to be getting drowsy.

'Call us any time, if you're worried,' Mavis insisted, before they said good night.

They had turned their light off and were settling down, when Reg said, 'We never mentioned the gas to her.'

'The what?' Mavis's voice was thick with sleep.

'The gas in the kitchen. To Miss Trubb.'

Mavis was awake again now.

'Nor we did. Neither did she, come to think of it. You'd have thought she might have said something. She must have turned it off.'

'Perhaps that was why she was still dressed.'

'It doesn't follow.'

'What doesn't?'

But Mavis had lost the thread. She was seeing again the stocky figure of Miss Trubb appearing from darkness.

'It was funny her light being off.'

'It was darned peculiar. Gave me quite a turn.'

'Same here. If she'd been in her nightdress it would have seemed natural. But like that, dressed and all, and not saying anything. . . .'

They were silent for a few seconds, then Reg said, in the casual voice he used to disguise anxieties, 'Hope she isn't going round the bend.'

'Do you think she might?'

'Well, what do we know about her? I mean, really know?'

'Only that she goes off to work in the City. She never goes out except to work. Not ever in the evenings, does she?'

'I've never known her go out. No friends at all, seemingly.'

'It *is* a bit queer. Why haven't we noticed it before?'

Reg laughed, an angry laugh.

'Because we were so bucked we had a paying lodger who did pay, didn't make rows, didn't mess up our things, and took on the baby-sitting.'

'That was it, I suppose.' Mavis was sinking again into

sleep. Reg heard her yawn, and stretched out a hand to pat her shoulder.

'It'll keep. I'll ask the old girl about the gas tomorrow morning, when I go round to fetch my things.'

'What things?'

'Brief-case and that. I didn't bother tonight.'

'You'll have to be up early to get through in time.'

'I'll be up. Don't you worry.'

Reg was awake at six, dressed, fed and ready to start at seven. In the end he had slept more soundly than Mavis, who had joined Carol about two in the morning, when Derek's fever seemed to have left him. They had changed his soaking sheets and given him clean pyjamas. Afterwards he slept, weak and exhausted, but comfortable at last. Mavis stayed awake till five, and then slept so heavily she did not hear Reg get up.

In fact the whole house was quiet when he left. The Fry children had not begun to chatter, and there was no sound from Joy. Reg drove off contentedly, sure that the crisis was over, and he would find his family at home after he got back from work, and everything as it should be.

He was wrong. The instant he opened his own front door he knew this. For it was a repetition of the night before, intensified. This time the gas assailed him at once in a choking wave, driving him back from the porch. He flung down his lighted cigarette and stamped it out. Then, taking a deep breath, ran straight through the house to the kitchen.

All the gas cooking-stove taps were on. The gas stung his eyes and his held breath was bursting his lungs. But he managed to turn off the taps and get back into the garden where he stood panting, dizzy and wondering what he ought to do next.

A neighbour, starting out to work, stopped to ask if anything was the matter. Reg stammered out his discovery. The neighbour looked surprised and curious. He joined Reg in the garden, looking up at the house. The latter understood.

'We weren't at home,' he explained. 'We were all – '

He broke off, appalled. Miss Trubb! He clutched the neighbour's arm.

'There's our lodger! It might have been her! I don't know if she's there!'

He started towards the door again, but the other pulled him back.

'You might never get up the stairs, and you don't even know if she's there. Haven't you got a ladder? Which is her room?'

More neighbours were gathering, drawn by the excited voices and gestures of the two men in the garden of Twenty-six. In less than ten minutes from the time Reg opened his front door, a ladder was brought and Miss Trubb's closed window was broken. She was discovered in her bed, unconscious but still breathing, and was carried rapidly downstairs into the garden. An ambulance was called, and the police. In a series of quick rushes all the doors and windows of the house were flung open. Gradually the smell of gas grew faint and disappeared.

After the ambulance had taken away Miss Trubb, the interested knot of people in the garden dispersed, feeling well satisfied with the morning's excitement. They had all done their best. The men were pleased with their own initiative and team work. The women were proud of their men. The casualty had not been too horrible to contemplate, and her fate was still undecided, and therefore interesting. They had enough to occupy their minds and conversation for the rest of the day.

As soon as he was allowed into the house, Reg rang up his firm to explain his absence, and after that Mavis, to tell her what had happened. She must stay at Carol's, he told her, and he would bring her home in the evening. Miss Trubb was in a pretty bad way, but she was still alive when the ambulance drove off, and they were going to give her an emergency transfusion as soon as they got her to the hospital, the St. John's men had said.

Mavis was too shocked to say much in answer to this news. The full implication would reach her slowly, Reg thought, as he turned from the telephone. It had only just begun to reach him. Detective-Inspector Brown, of the local C.I.D., found a very thoughtful man standing in his garden, staring at his widely open house. The constable who had arrived with

Brown took up a position outside the gate, to move on the fresh batch of spectators that was gathering in purely idle curiosity.

'Do you want to go in?' Reg asked, with a faint grin. 'The hall's all right. I've been on the phone.'

'Not at present. I'd just like to hear your version of what happened.'

Reg told him. He explained why he and his family had been away from home for the night.

'What worries me most,' he went on, 'is the gas the first time.'

Brown was startled.

'What d'you mean by that?'

'My wife noticed a faint smell of gas when we came back for our things, and to fetch Joy, our little girl. I checked the taps. They were all off. But the smell was definite in the kitchen, and faint in the hall. I opened the window in the kitchen to let it out. The wall ventilator was working, of course. There was no smell at all upstairs. We thought Miss Trubb had let something boil over, and a bit of gas had escaped, and she'd turned it off all right.'

'Did you ask her?'

'No.'

'Did you see any evidence of anything having boiled over? Any mess on the stove?'

'No. I didn't think of it when I was in the kitchen. It was Mavis's idea, but she didn't go to look, either.'

'You say you opened the kitchen window?'

'Yes. I did.'

'Was it still open this morning?'

Reg was astounded.

'No. No, of course it wasn't. How could it be? The place was full of gas.'

'You definitely saw the window was shut?'

'Not when I went in to turn off the taps. I thought I'd never make it. Not on one breath. I concentrated on getting the taps off, and getting back out.'

Brown nodded, smiling approval. This young man had guts and he had sense. The two did not always go together.

'Can we look at the kitchen from the outside?'

'Sure.'

They walked round the house. Both halves of the kitchen window had been broken. The glass lay on the path and on the narrow flower bed under the window. Many feet had trampled the bed and the grass beyond the path. The empty window frames lay back against the wall of the house on either side, unhooked.

'You're insured, I hope,' said the Inspector, dryly.

'Yes, I'm insured.'

'That's a bit odd,' said Brown. He pointed at the wall. A large piece of moss was clinging to it. Reg stared.

'That's the outside of the ventilator,' he said. 'I wonder how the moss got there?'

The Inspector nodded, and they walked on round the house. Reg pointed to Miss Trubb's window, also broken. The ladder brought by a neighbour was still leaning against the wall outside it.

Inspector Brown climbed the ladder. He pushed back the broken window, and wrapping a scarf, which he took from his pocket, about the lower part of his face, leaned into the room.

The bed was in disorder and a small table and chair near it had been overturned in the haste to get Miss Trubb out of that poisonous place. Otherwise the room was tidy. The victim's clothes lay in an ordered heap on the top of a chest of drawers. Her dressing-table was neatly arranged. The inspector saw no sign of any letter or other form of message. Very soon he withdrew his head, removed the scarf, and went back down the ladder.

'I'll have to have a look round inside when the air clears,' he said. 'I wouldn't stay any time indoors yet if I were you. The monoxide sinks, as it's heavier than air, so the ground floor is the worst. Leave it a few hours. I've got someone on guard. You needn't worry.'

'I'm not worried,' Reg said, slightly resenting the paternal tone. 'I've already arranged to pick up my family this evening. But I need some papers for my job. I suppose I can go in for my brief-case?'

'Ground floor?'

'Hall table.'

'O.K. If you don't dawdle.'

Reg had no wish to dawdle. The hall still held a faint smell of gas, but less than when he had used the telephone. He whipped up his brief-case and was out of the house again in a matter of seconds. He wanted to get on to the works.

'Is it in order to ring up the hospital?' he asked Brown, as they moved together towards the gate.

'Yes, if you want to.'

'Of course I want to. We *liked* her. I'd never have thought – Well, I mean to say – *suicide!* What for, for heaven's sake? She always acted so sensibly.'

The Inspector made no answer at all.

'Is it O.K. to see about getting those windows done?' Reg asked, as Brown remained silent.

'I'll see to it for you,' the latter answered, unexpectedly. 'I want to have a good look round before anything is altered. But we'll have you all secure by tonight. Don't worry.'

Again the younger man was inclined to resent this friendliness, as some form of patronage. But the Inspector's manner was disarming, and he found himself grinning his thanks instead.

Reg found Miss Trubb's note in his brief-case when he reached his desk in the designers' room at the works. It was in an envelope, pinned to another envelope. It read, 'Please deliver the enclosed, and God bless you, all three.' The enclosure, the other envelope, was addressed to: 'Mrs Frances Meadows, Downside, London Road, Weyford, Surrey.' It was neither sealed nor stamped.

Reg looked at it for some minutes, considering what he should do. There was something very queer about this. Miss Trubb gave no explanation in her note to him, but presumably there was something in the letter to Mrs Meadows, whoever she might be. And this letter was open. By accident, or by design? And if the latter, why such an indirect way of explaining – what?

The ordinary rules of behaviour did not apply here, Reg decided. He wanted to know why Miss Trubb had tried to gas herself. After all, she had used his house for the attempt, with all sorts of unpleasant consequences for him and his family, and they were not at the end of them yet. He had a right to know. Mavis, too. Perhaps he ought to hand the whole thing to Inspector Brown. But he remembered that though Brown had asked a lot of questions and seemed to be making very heavy weather of the whole affair, he had not offered any explanation at all of his keen interest in Miss Trubb. Did an ordinary suicide always induce such an attitude, such detailed sleuthing? Reg did not know, but he thought the letter to Mrs Meadows might enlighten him. He took it out of the envelope and read it.

At the end of the day, when he collected Mavis and Joy from the Frys' house, where Derek was sitting up, restored and penitent for all the trouble he had caused, he showed the letter to his wife and friends.

'It doesn't really say anything,' Carol concluded, handing it back to Reg.

'Just says she is going away where she will never trouble her again,' Mavis said, thoughtfully. 'That must mean suicide. I wonder who Frances is.'

'One of those relations or friends we never saw or heard of,' Reg suggested.

'Could be. Anyway, there's the address. We can sent on the letter and write ourselves at the same time.'

Derek stretched out a hand.

'Let's have another look,' he said. He held the single page by one corner, between finger and thumb, moving it from side to side.

'I'd say it was written by a definitely unstable character,' he decided. 'Pencil, to start with. You'd expect a woman of her age with a long secretarial experience to have a pen, most likely a ball pen. And then why cut the edge of the paper into a wavy line?'

Reg took it back from him.

'I noticed that, but I thought it was the kind of paper. Fancy type.'

'Wavy on one side only?'

Mavis laughed, snatching the letter from Reg.

'He's right, darling. She must have done it. But of course she was mentally unstable. We were only saying last evening – '

'She was holding a pencil!' Reg broke in. 'My God, she was writing this note when we came back!'

Mavis's face whitened.

'She must have started before we came! That gas smell! She must have started, and turned it off when she heard us. *And Joy was in the house!*'

There was a horrified silence, broken in the end by Reg.

'I don't believe it went like that,' he said. 'I don't really believe she was round the bend. We've had her in the house for nearly six months, and I've never met a saner person. Reserved, I grant you. But not mental. Nowhere near it.'

'It's very difficult to tell,' Carol began, and Derek added, 'Doesn't the suicide attempt prove it?'

But Reg was obstinate. He took his family home, where they found a constable still on guard. Temporary boards had been nailed over the broken windows, and the rooms were in some disorder, after the police search, but the house was free from gas, and perfectly safe.

Mavis was inclined to be tearful over the state of her home, but Reg's thoughts were elsewhere.

'I'll just drop round to the hospital,' he said. 'I'd rather give this note to the doctor than to the police. If he hands it on, that's his responsibility. I suppose if she hasn't pulled round, it'll be for the coroner.'

But he found that Miss Trubb had made progress, though she was still critically ill. He was not allowed to see her, and the doctor in charge was working in another part of the hospital, but the Ward Sister took him into her room and looked at the envelope, without taking out its contents, and promised to show it to the doctor later.

'I shan't have to post it,' she said, 'because Mrs Meadows will be here this evening. She is Miss Trubb's sister.'

Reg was astonished.

'How did you find that out? Is she conscious?'

'Not properly. She can't tell us anything yet.'

'Then how?'

'It was the police,' Sister told him. 'They gave me the name and address, and said to send for Mrs Meadows.'

'The *police?*'

Sister pursed her lips.

'In cases of attempted suicide the police attend, to take a statement if the patient recovers. It's still a crime, you know.'

'Yes, but – ' Reg was exasperated. 'These days, it's always mental, isn't it? I thought the law was out, in most cases.'

'The police are not called in a good many cases,' said Sister, with some asperity, for she disliked having a member of the Force in her ward. 'You called them, I understand.'

'My neighbours did,' said Reg. 'Interfering so-and-so's.'

Sister remained calm.

'Perhaps you'd like to have a word with the officer,' she suggested.

Reg hesitated.

'The letter,' he began, and stopped.

'I will give the letter to Mrs Meadows,' Sister repeated firmly. 'The letter is nobody's business but Miss Trubb's and her sister's.'

Reg, blushing deeply, followed her into the ward.

The constable on duty came out of the cubicle, stared suspiciously at Reg, and waited for the young man to begin. But when the latter explained who he was, his manner altered and became almost confidential.

'You were darned lucky, son,' he confided. 'Coming back when you did. You were all well out of it, in the circumstances.'

'I don't understand,' cried Reg. 'All these hints and mysteries! Was it suicide or wasn't it? And how did you find out so quickly about this Meadows woman being her sister?'

He was appalled at what he had just said. The constable's eyes narrowed.

'How do *you* know about Mrs Meadows?'

Sister came to the rescue.

'I told him,' she said quietly, 'that Miss Trubb's sister was on her way. I must say I wondered myself how you people knew. But of course you've been through her things in her room, I suppose.'

At this point the constable committed his big indiscretion. The temptation was great and he succumbed to it.

'We didn't have to look far,' he said. 'We know Miss Trubb. We know her very well. We've known her for over fifteen years.'

18

CHAPTER 3

Mrs Meadows arrived at the hospital at half-past nine that evening. The Ward Sister had gone off duty, but the night nurse installed her in Sister's room and told the Night Sister of her arrival. The latter came quickly in answer to the summons. Miss Frubb's case was unusual, rather disquieting. All of the hospital staff, from the consultants downwards, were prepared to treat it as something very special. Consequently Miss Trubb's sister, her only surviving near relative, was someone very special, too.

'I'm sorry to keep you waiting, Mrs Meadows,' Night Sister told her. 'I hope Nurse has been looking after you.'

'Yes, indeed,' answered the visitor, moving her hand in a comprehensive gesture towards the cup of tea on the small table beside her, and the glow of the electric fire beyond. 'And really you have been no time at all.'

Night Sister looked at her with approval. A woman in her late thirties, she judged, or perhaps a well-preserved woman of forty-two or three. Handsome, with dark auburn hair, showing no touches of grey, quite well-made clothes, reasonably fashionable. Very different from the elderly, shapeless Miss Trubb, she thought. And then she pulled herself up. The unfortunate creature in Bed Twenty was not looking her normal self. She was desperately ill, clinging to life now with a tenacity all the more surprising for her recent presumed rejection of it.

'How is my sister?' Mrs Meadows asked quietly.

If Night Sister had been less preoccupied with her comparisons she might have been surprised by the gentle resignation of the other's manner, which expressed no deeper emotion than a mild anxiety.

'Holding her own. We are amazed that she has pulled through so far.'

Mrs Meadows sighed.

'Perhaps I ought not to say this. But for her own sake I almost wish – '

She broke off, lifting troubled, candid eyes to search her companion's face.

Night Sister pulled forward a chair and sat down. She had her normal share of natural curiosity. It was no crime, she thought, to get ahead of her colleague in the matter of Miss Trubb's history.

'Your sister has been – unfortunate?' she asked, with the maximum of awkward tact.

Long years had hardened Mrs Meadows. She replied, mechanically, 'My sister has served fifteen years in prison; a life sentence.'

'For – ' began Sister, and could not finish.

'For murder,' answered Mrs Meadows, in the same quiet voice.

'Oh! I – I'm sorry,' said Night Sister, and sat staring at the visitor.

They had all suspected some former trouble with the police. The Ward Sister had spread the news of the constable's remark to Reg Holmes. But they had all concluded that poor Miss Trubb must be one of those petty thieves, kleptomaniacs really, because they couldn't help it, who *would* go on snatching things from shops, and getting caught. A series of convictions was what they had all decided upon. A series of short sentences. And then a sudden burst of enlightenment, of self-awareness, and self-disgust, and an impulse to end it all.

Night Sister remembered. She had been given an envelope to hand to Mrs Meadows when she arrived. She did so now.

'This was found,' she said. 'Miss Trubb left it with the owner of the house where she has been living. He brought it up here.'

Mrs Meadows took it, rather reluctantly, Sister thought.

'Perhaps he ought to have given it to the police,' she said.

'I think he wanted to avoid that. It was addressed to you and had been slipped into his brief-case, a place the police would not look for it. So he brought it to the hospital.'

'I wonder if I ought to hand it on,' Mrs Meadows repeated, still looking at the outside of the envelope.

'Aren't you going to read it first?'

'I suppose I must.'

She drew out the single sheet of paper and Sister watched her eyes moving down the page. For a few seconds Mrs Meadows sat with bowed head. Then she covered her face with her hands, and her thin body shook with silent tears.

'There, there,' Night Sister said, getting up to pat her shoulder. 'It's not your fault the poor thing is out of her mind.'

Mrs Meadows sat up, fumbling for a handkerchief.

'Is that what they think?' she said, trying to control herself. 'Is that what they think at last?'

A nurse looked in to say that Night Sister was wanted in Ward Seven.

'I'll come back,' the latter told Mrs Meadows. 'I won't be long. Nurse will look after you.'

'Can't I see Helen?'

'Helen?'

'My sister. Helen Clements. She calls herself Trubb, but her name is Clements.'

'Oh. Well, just wait till I come back. I won't be long.'

Mrs Meadows nodded, and Night Sister hurried away. She still had the situation in her own hands, she was pleased to think, thanks to the co-operative, submissive attitude of Miss Trubb's sister. Poor woman, what a thing to have in the family! It was the first time Sister had come across the near relation of a murderess. And the murderess herself, she remembered, with a little excited shudder.

She solved the problem in Ward Seven at high speed, and was back again in less than twenty minutes.

She found Mrs Meadows in the passage to the ward, talking to the constable on duty. She felt an instant alarm for her nurses.

'Is it safe to leave her, officer?' she asked, severely.

The man looked surprised.

'I wouldn't know,' he said. 'I'm not the doctor.'

'I didn't mean from the medical point of view,' Sister snapped, annoyed by this misunderstanding. 'I'm thinking of my nurses. Are they safe to be alone with her?'

The policeman's face reddened slowly. He had followed his orders most carefully. Except for the slip when he talked to Reg Holmes, he had let out nothing. That must have been enough. They must have guessed. Or had the Press been snooping already? She hadn't changed her name again, unluckily for her. Surprising, too. He wondered why she had not taken such an obvious precaution against being identified.

'I told Sister something about my sister's history,' said Mrs Meadows, in her gentle sensible voice. 'I thought it was only fair to the hospital.' Her fine eyes were turned up to the constable's face now. They filled with tears as she spoke, and he watched the tears begin to run down her cheeks. His embarrassment grew. All these women! He turned to Night Sister.

'Miss Trubb seems to be asleep,' he said. 'Nurse told me she was sleeping naturally, and she'd keep an eye on her while I slipped out for a cuppa. Then Mrs Meadows – '

'I heard his voice,' explained Miss Trubb's sister. 'So I left the waiting-room. . . .'

'Sister's room.'

Night Sister was tired of these explanations. There was no point in them.

'I'm sorry. Sister's room. To see if he could tell me exactly what happened. I don't suppose any of you know at the hospital.'

'Mr Holmes, the owner of the house, gave Sister a detailed account,' said Night Sister, 'which she passed on to me. I could have told you if you'd asked me.'

'You were called away,' said Mrs Meadows, reasonably and apologetically.

The constable, meanwhile, had faded into the ward kitchen, where a probationer on night duty had his tea waiting for him.

'Perhaps you would like just a glimpse of your sister before you go,' said Night Sister, stiffly. Discipline must be restored, and the reins of the whole situation gathered back into her

22

own hands. It was clear that Mrs Meadows must be tired and anxious to reach her hotel, or wherever she was staying.

'I hope you have arranged somewhere to stay,' said Sister as they moved towards the ward door.

'Yes, thank you.'

Night Sister led the way to Miss Trubb's cubicle and passed inside the curtain. The patient was alone, very quiet, breathing normally, her colour much improved. She was drowsy, but not asleep. Her eyes, which had been staring vacantly into the distance, focused on Night Sister, without recognition, but with intelligence.

'Miss Trubb,' said Sister, feeling rather queer, for the total ordinariness of the patient destroyed her recently-built, melo-dramatic fantasies, 'there's someone to see you, dear.'

She was horrified with herself for using the habitual kindly manner of speech to such a person, but it had escaped her from force of habit. She turned round to motion Mrs Meadows forward, but the latter was already inside the cubicle, and Sister did not see the change come over Miss Trubb's face.

But she heard the harsh intake of her breath, and as she turned again quickly towards the bed, saw Miss Trubb half raised on one elbow, with the other hand beating the air between her and her sister.

'Frances!' Miss Trubb whispered. 'Frances! For God's sake leave me alone! For God's sake – '

She sank back on the pillow. As Night Sister darted forward she heard behind her Mrs Meadows sobbing, 'Poor Helen! Oh, poor Helen, why does she have to go on living?'

Reg was not altogether surprised, when he got back to Sand-fields Avenue from the hospital, to find a Press reporter sitting with Mavis, eagerly taking down her account of Miss Trubb's strangeness the night before. The reporter, a middle-aged man with a thin face and thinner hair, got up nervously when Reg walked in.

'This gentleman is from the *Daily Splash*,' Mavis explained. 'I told him I wasn't here this morning, but he wants to know anything we noticed about Miss Trubb.'

'Why?' asked Reg.

'In the public interest,' the reporter said, quickly, eager to remove the belligerent expression that had spread over Reg's face.

'Interest, my foot,' the latter answered. 'Morbid curiosity, if you ask me. What have you told him?' he asked Mavis, in a voice of quite unusual severity.

'The truth,' she answered, stoutly. She was not going to be bullied before strangers, even by Reg.

'Then see you don't alter it,' he told the reporter. 'You may as well know we thought a lot of Miss Trubb. We've nothing against her, whatever she's done.'

'What has she done?' cried Mavis, exasperated. 'He keeps hinting, and now you! I don't know how he expects me to remember what was in the papers nearly sixteen years ago. I didn't take all that notice of them at eight years of age, as I told him. Perhaps you did. You were twelve, weren't you?'

'I don't say I remember any Miss Trubb. I wasn't interested, except in the football. But you seem to know something about her, like the copper up at the hospital. "We've known her for over fifteen years." That's what he said. Well, what about it? Suppose she has been in trouble, off and on? She wasn't in trouble with us. She paid her rent, and she never took anything that I've missed. Have you missed anything?' he asked Mavis, rounding on her suddenly.

'Of course not. You'd have soon heard of it if I had.'

'So what?' Reg asked the reporter.

The latter, who had already approached one or two neighbours for an account of the actual discovery of the suicide attempt, put away his note-book and stood up. Mavis had given him ample material for his story, he decided. Reg had confirmed some of it. The 'innocent victims' angle was well established. Better get back now and write it up. It was front page stuff. Mustn't keep them waiting. There was just the picture —

He walked across to the window that opened on to the garden, raising his hand in a sweeping gesture towards the trim rose beds on the little trampled lawn.

'Nice place you've got,' he said.

He turned back. The camera man beyond the hedge moved round to cover the front door.

'I'll be getting along now,' the reporter said. 'Many thanks for your co-operation.'

'You haven't given us the gen on Miss Trubb,' Reg protested.

'Buy the paper in the morning,' the man answered, with a slow wink. Everything had gone well. There was only the picture —

Reg opened the door. Mavis stood back. Obviously they were not going outside with him. The reporter moved on, saying, 'There was just one more thing, Mr Holmes. . . .'

He spoke quietly, too quietly for Reg to hear properly.

'Pardon?' the latter said from the door. The reporter continued to murmur, so Reg followed him, trying to catch what he was saying.

Mavis hesitated, thought she heard Joy whimper, and, glad of the excuse, ran lightly upstairs. When the magnesium flare lit the dusk with its unnatural brilliance she thought for a second that it was lightning. Immediately afterwards she heard the front door slam shut, and Reg's voice calling to her.

'Bloody bastard!' he shouted. 'Good job you stayed behind! He didn't get what he wanted!'

This was true. The picture was a flop. They had reckoned on securing startled expressions on the two young faces when the flare went off. Startled expressions, good for a caption on the lines of 'This is terrible! If we had not come back!' Or, 'My baby! Alone in the house with her!' Or something else of the sort. As it was, the film merely showed the reporter looking thinner than ever, and Reg's back in full flight. Quite useless.

The Holmeses did not take the *Daily Splash* as a rule, but Reg bought one on his way to work and Mavis when she went out shopping. They were both appalled by what they found. Reg rang up Mavis at lunch time. He could tell from her voice that she had been crying.

'You mustn't let it upset you too much,' he said, gently. 'Think of Joy.'

'I am. All the time. We left her alone in the house with that — with a *child murderer!*'

Her voice had gone up dangerously high. She was on the verge of hysteria, he decided.

'Look,' he said. 'Why don't you go round to Carol's this afternoon? Unload it on her. She won't mind. You'll make yourself ill if you go on thinking it over alone.'

'I feel ill now. I feel sick every time I look at that photo of her.'

'It was taken sixteen years ago. And listen. That reporter has twisted your statements as I expected. I can't explain over the phone, but I will when I get back. I'll get off a bit early if I can. You go over to Carol's. The walk'll do you good. Be home to cook my tea, though. Don't be late. 'Bye!'

He was back from the works earlier than usual. Everyone there had been sympathetic, if a trifle subdued. With the usual hind-sight they all thought he had been very rash to take a lodger without references. Of course it was unusual to land a criminal, especially one of such notoriety as Miss Trubb. The older men could not understand his failing to identify her, since she still used the name by which she was known at her trial. On the other hand his own contemporaries assured Reg that they had never heard of her, or the case either. *The Daily Splash* had probably blown it up, anyhow.

'You needn't take all that for gospel,' Reg told Mavis when, their meal over and washed up, they sat down to discuss their lodger.

'I've moved Joy's cot into our bedroom,' said Mavis. Reg got up to kiss her.

'Silly darling. Nothing can harm her.'

'I don't know so much. It makes me shiver just to think of our ignorance all these weeks and months.'

'Well, for one thing, they've got their facts wrong. Just to build up a sensation. "Child murderess repeats her crime." "Foiled by father!" That's all tripe.'

'Why? There was gas in the house when we came back. She hadn't gone to bed.'

'The taps were all off.'

'She did that when she heard us.'

'I doubt it. You can't prove it, anyway.'

'You can't prove she didn't.'

'Well, she didn't act guilty when we knocked her up.'

'I don't know so much. She acted very strange. It gave us both a turn. You know it did.'

'I admit I was surprised to see her dressed and the light off in her room. But she may have wanted us to think she had gone to bed.'

'So she could gas the lot of us.'

'It wasn't us,' Reg insisted. 'She gassed herself. She knew we'd all gone. Come to think of it, she looked quite pleased when we said we were going. I think she was glad to have us all out of the way. I don't believe, and I never will believe, she meant to harm Joy.'

'I don't know what to believe,' Mavis said, miserably. 'I wish we'd never set eyes on her in the first place.'

Reg took his wife on his knee. She buried her face in his shoulder and cried, while he stroked her hair, talking quietly all the time, more to himself than to her.

'That note she wrote to her sister, and hid in my brief-case. I think she was writing it when we came back. So she meant to do something then. Just go away, perhaps. That was all it said. Creep out of the house when we were asleep.'

'If we'd been here we'd have been gassed, too.'

'No. Don't you see, that idea might have come to her *after we left*. She must have seen we were startled. She'd be afraid we thought she was getting mental and we'd make inquiries and then everything would come out. And she couldn't face it. So she decided to end it all.'

Mavis sat up, drying her eyes.

'Perhaps they'd found out at the place where she worked, and made things unpleasant for her. Or someone might have tried to blackmail her. She never had any visitors that I knew of. But when we were out, anyone might have called.'

'We could ask round if any of the neighbours saw anyone call when we were out.'

'It would look rather peculiar, wouldn't it? We don't know many to ask, do we?'

'I'll try Mr Burridge. I ought to go round and thank him for the loan of the ladder, anyway.'

Mavis agreed to that. She foresaw a lot of unwelcome popularity waiting for her in the shopping centre. Already people she did not know had made opportunities to speak.

Others had given her hostile critical glances, as much as to say, 'If your child had been murdered you'd only have yourself to blame.' But she would make what capital she could out of all this. If it would help to clear up the mystery of Miss Trubb's action, it would be worth it.

'We still mind about her a lot, don't we?' she said, looking deep into Reg's eyes. His own answered with instant recognition of this feeling.

'We do. I rang up the hospital today. She's better. Out of danger, they said. Her sister's been, and gone back to Weyford.'

'How do you know where she comes from?'

'It was on the envelope. Didn't I say?'

'I forgot.'

Mavis yawned. She was suddenly tired of Miss Trubb. They would never see her again, whatever happened, whatever she had done or not done. The doctors would take care of her now, poor old thing.

'I suppose they'll send her to a mental hospital after this lot,' she said, sleepily, getting up from her husband's knee and walking away to another chair. 'Gosh, I'm tired!'

'So you ought to be,' Reg agreed. 'Bed's the place, for both of us. We haven't had much sleep for two nights, come to think of it.'

But as they went upstairs he said, slowly, his thoughts still on their former lodger, 'You know, somehow I don't think she's mental. There's a lot I'd like to know about our Miss Trubb.'

'Well, really!' Mavis exclaimed, crossly. '*Our* Miss Trubb, indeed! Can't we forget her, for heaven's sake? Now it's all over!'

CHAPTER 4

But it was not all over, certainly not for Reg, nor, reluctantly, following his lead, for Mavis. It was only just beginning.

The Holmeses took the unwelcome publicity quietly, with distaste, but with patience. So unsensational was their attitude that the Press soon wearied of them, to pursue more lively subjects. Reg and Mavis settled into a new routine, without their lodger. And very gradually, as the days passed, they learned how much she had done for them, how much they had grown to rely on her commonsense and balanced judgment, in how many ways she had supported and helped them, particularly Mavis, in the small everyday problems of living.

Outwardly all was as it had been. The windows were mended, the trampled garden restored to its former trim appearance, all signs of the disturbance and violence of that unhappy morning had vanished. From severe criticism of the young people's rashness in harbouring a criminal, the neighbours had passed to a more charitable view. Mavis was greeted, not with contemptuous or outraged expressions of censure, but with sympathetic congratulations on her family's narrow escape, and a vague tolerant assurance that 'you never know, do you?'

Mavis thought she did know, but she said nothing to her acquaintances, only to Reg.

'I miss her!' she cried, towards the end of the second week. 'I can't help but miss her. Every time I go to look in her room, I see her sitting there, so sort of peaceful she always was in the evening. You could tell her anything. She took

29

such a real interest. Child murder! It simply doesn't make sense!'

'I agree,' Reg said firmly. He waited for a few seconds, then went on, 'I took her things up to the hospital today, and do you know what?'

'Go on.'

'She put the rent she owed us for the half week in an envelope, addressed to me. I wanted to see her and thank her, but Sister said she wouldn't see anyone. Not even her sister. Got all worked up the first night this Mrs Meadows was at the hospital. They didn't dare let her stay, and she hasn't been back since.'

'That's the one that lives in Weyford?'

'That's right.'

'She could tell us.'

'How d'you mean?'

'She could tell us the whole story. What really happened.'

'We know what happened.'

'In the first place, stupid. When she's supposed to have killed a child.'

Reg looked at his wife with keen eyes.

'So you're coming round to my point of view, are you? You don't believe she'd do any such thing?'

'It's very hard to believe. I tell you, every time I go in her room – '

'I know. I know. The last person on earth to kill anyone, let alone a child. I'm pretty well convinced of it.'

'Not that we really do know,' Mavis said, thoughtfully. 'It's all very well having opinions, but you ought to go by the facts, oughtn't you?'

Reg nodded. He had been bitterly disappointed at the hospital by his failure to see Miss Trubb. Vaguely, he had imagined himself persuading her to confide in him. After all, she owed them an explanation. Her total refusal, added to her painstaking honesty in the matter of the rent, baffled him. Unless, and always you had to come back to it, she was up the wall, as so many of them hinted.

'I even got hold of her doctor,' he told Mavis, pursuing his own line of thought. 'Young chap, very considerate and all that. But not giving anything away. The psychiatrist was seeing her. That was all he said. No verdict on her mental state at present. Slow recovery. Danger of pneumonia. She seemed listless and not interested in her surroundings. Mustn't be excited or roused emotionally. In plain English, don't be nosey, and get the hell out.'

'Well, I suppose she's every right to cut herself off if she wants to. I don't believe she's mental, but I don't see how anyone could suffer as she has without being altered. Imagine being shut up for fifteen years!'

'A life sentence with full remissions,' said Reg, grimly. 'She must have behaved herself all along, mustn't she?'

'Don't be horrible!'

They left it there for that evening, but by the next night Reg had decided upon action. While Mavis was washing up the supper things, he got out writing block and envelopes and composed a letter to Mrs Meadows. When Mavis joined him, he showed it to her before sealing it up.

'She can hardly refuse to tell us the story,' Mavis said. 'Unless she simply refers us back to the newspapers. But you've made it pretty clear you don't trust Press accounts, haven't you? She may just write back, of course. Do you really think she'll see us?'

'The way I've put it, she might.'

'But we don't *have* any friends in those parts! You make it sound very posh,' Mavis said, giggling. 'Asked to lunch with family friends near Weyford. Reg, you have got a nerve!'

'Why not? One of our directors lives out that way.'

'And he's asked us to lunch, I suppose?'

They both laughed.

'If it's a nice day we'll take sandwiches and have lunch on the downs. Far better than in anybody's house. Then we can look up this Mrs Meadows afterwards.'

'If she asks us.'

'I think she will. From what Sister said she was only too anxious to help. She's been out of touch since Miss Trubb came out of the nick. She probably wants to know what we can tell her.'

He was right. Mrs Meadows answered the letter by return of post, thanking him for taking the trouble to write, and saying she would be most happy to see him and his wife the following Sunday, any time during the afternoon. They were not to hurry from their lunch party. She had no other engagement. She ended the letter with a careful description of how to reach her house.

Reg and Mavis arrived there about three o'clock on the following Sunday afternoon. They had no difficulty in finding the place, which was on the outskirts of the town, with a ridge of down visible from the road, but some distance off. 'Downside' was not a true description of the house, as Mavis pointed out. There was a drive leading in to the front door, but Reg stopped in the road just short of it.

'Ought we to drive in?' he asked.

Mavis was surprised at this diffidence.

'Why ever not? Of course, drive in. The gate's open. Joy's asleep. We can't leave her out in the road here, but we could leave her in the car in the drive.'

This sensible argument prevailed. Reg drove in and stopped near the front door. A slim woman in a becoming wool dress of misty blue appeared at once on the steps.

'Of course you mustn't disturb the baby,' she said, when they had introduced themselves, and Mavis had put her problem.

'What a pet!' she exclaimed, peering into the carry-cot through the rear window. 'And so good. Fast asleep, bless her!'

She led them into the house, which was solid, Victorian, ugly on the outside, but spacious and well-furnished within. Taking them into her large drawing-room she moved at once to the big sash windows, opening one of them at the bottom.

'There,' she said, 'if the wee girlie cries out, we shall hear her at once. I don't think we shall find it too cold.'

Her voice and manner of speaking were not unlike Miss Trubb's, Mavis decided, but her circumstances were obviously very different indeed.

'Now make yourselves at home,' Mrs Meadows went on, pointing to various large and ornately-covered armchairs. 'I must say, straight away, I was very grateful to you for writing. I want you to tell me all you know about poor Helen, from

32

the time she went to live with you. You see, we lost sight of her completely from the moment she was – set free.'

Mrs Meadows lowered her voice on the last two words, and looked down at her clasped hands. Her manner was wholly restrained, but Reg, seeing her knuckles whiten, understood the feeling she suppressed.

'We thought a lot of Miss Trubb,' he said, gently. 'In a way, we still do.'

Mrs Meadows looked up, an incredulous light in her eyes.

'You are very generous,' she murmured, and stopped, apparently too overcome to continue.

Mavis began to speak. Her account of their recent lodger was rambling and confused and repetitious, but the general opinion behind it was borne in upon Mrs Meadows with considerable force. These young Holmeses could not believe in Helen's crime. They wanted to hear the full story.

When Reg added his own quota of observation and conclusion, Frances Meadows sat up very straight in her chair.

'I think it is wonderful to find young people like yourselves so forgiving and so anxious to think well of others. Poor Helen has not come in contact with many like you. On the contrary, from the start the great majority were willing, even eager, to believe in her guilt.'

'Did *you* believe in it?' Reg asked, suddenly and quite bluntly.

Mrs Meadows's face grew a shade paler, but her gentle voice was not changed as she said, 'Most unwillingly. Most unwillingly. But the facts were there. And she would not help herself. In the end I came to believe she *could* not help herself.'

'Couldn't help doing it?' Mavis asked. She had not understood what Mrs Meadows was trying to say.

'No, no. Or perhaps that, too,' Mrs Meadows went on. 'No, I mean she could not produce any evidence in her favour, and that was why she refused to help her solicitor and her counsel.'

Seeing that a look of bewilderment persisted on the faces of her two visitors, Mrs Meadows said, 'I will tell you the whole story from the beginning, and then you must judge for yourselves. But there is, I'm afraid, and always has been, only one conclusion in this sad, sad business.'

She got out her handkerchief and blew her nose, and then, still sitting upright and unrelaxed, her eyes fixed upon the wall opposite, she told her story, in a quiet unvaried voice. Every word bit into their understanding, slowly, relentlessly, destroying the picture of Miss Trubb as they had come to know and like and admire her.

Helen, two years older than her sister Frances, was born and brought up in Weyford. Her father had a business in the town, inheriting it in turn from his father. The family circle, of shop keepers, builders and so on, was widely known and respected. When the two girls were in their teens, Mrs Clements died, to the great grief of all who had known her. Mr Clements did not marry again, and the role of housekeeper and hostess in the home fell to Helen's lot, as the elder, together with the care of her younger sister. Both girls attended the local High School and did well there. Helen went on to a secretarial college in the town, with a view to entering her father's business. He had been disappointed of a son to follow him, but Helen's ability promised a capable secretary, if not, later on, a partner.

For one year Helen worked in the business. Frances, whose tastes were different, was at this time attending a small art school, though her talent, as she readily confessed, was not remarkable.

This was in 1939. By the end of the year Helen was practically indispensable to her father, who had already lost to the Forces two of his most promising clerks.

It was in February of 1940 that Helen suddenly left home to take up work in Conington. Frances said she would always remember the day Helen announced her decision. There had been no warning of her intention; no discussion, no argument. She simply told her father she had arranged to go to a new job, in a factory in Conington. It was war work. She did not want to wait until she was called up, and sent just anywhere. She was going now. The next day she had gone.

Mr Clements took months to recover from the shock of this deceitful desertion, as he regarded it. Helen was his standby. She had all the qualities of steady concentration, level-headedness and loyalty, that her mother had possessed so abundantly. He simply could not understand it, and blamed it on the war, which was unsettling everyone, and on the fact that his business was not directly concerned with any part of the war effort. But it hurt him unbearably that she had not seen fit to consult him, or even give him reasonable warning of her intention, before she left.

Frances continued to be very worried. She, too, had been shocked by her sister's action, and understood it no better than her father. So, after two months had passed, she went to Comington to see Helen. Her worst fears were realized. She found her sister five months gone in pregnancy, wearing a wedding ring bought at Woolworth's, and calling herself Mrs Trubb. Her landlady, before Frances's visit, had been given to understand that she had a husband in the Army. Frances, in her innocence, destroyed that myth by asking for Miss Clements, and afterwards Helen moved to another address, giving up the pretence of marriage, but keeping the name of Trubb. Frances arranged to visit her from time to time, and to be with her, if she was still free herself, when the baby was born. At this time she was not at home, but attached to a unit providing camouflage on buildings in various parts of the country.

Meanwhile she agreed to keep the facts from her father. This was not difficult. She was not seeing much of him, and his early shock and grief had been replaced now by anger. He did not want to hear anything about his elder daughter. She did not choose to write to him, or to any of her former friends. Very well. He washed his hands of her.

But there was one former friend who caused some embarrassment to Frances. This was one of her father's younger clerks, a very promising young man, who had left to join the Army soon after war broke out. Colin Meadows had been friendly with Helen, whom he saw daily in the Clements office. Indeed Frances, with schoolgirl or rather student fantasy, had imagined a budding romance between them. Certainly for a time Colin tried to keep in touch with Helen, and confided his hurt feelings to Frances when he had no success in doing so. Gradually she became aware that his visits to their house on his leaves always coincided with her own, and were made on her account, not her sister's. But two months after her first visit to Helen, she herself moved to Conington, to be near her sister during her ordeal. She took war work in a factory there.

Helen's baby was born, without difficulty or complications. Frances went home again and joined the W.A.A.F. A year later still she married Colin Meadows, and told him Helen's secret, which he promised to keep from her father and friends in Weyford.

When the big raids began in the autumn of 1940, soon after the baby was born, Helen was bombed out of her lodgings, and moved to another part of the town. Frances sent her money from time to time, but she did not really need it, as she was earning very good wages in the secretarial section of a war factory, and there were the usual allowances for the child and herself, and a crèche where the baby could stay during her working hours. There were only too many girls at that time in Helen's predicament, Frances said, sadly.

In 1943 Mr Clements died, rather suddenly. It was a cancer, Frances explained, not suspected by anyone until an emergency operation became necessary. He died two days later. Colin, invalided out of the Forces after being badly wounded, took over the business as soon as he was fit. It had been left in its entirety to Frances. Her sister was not mentioned in the will.

A month after her father's death Helen's little boy was found dead, suffocated in his cot. The child was three; there was no question of an accident. He had been killed deliberately. Helen was arrested and charged with the murder.

And now, for the first time, she denied parentage of the child. She said she was looking after the boy for a friend, a girl in the Forces, who paid her for doing so. She also denied murdering the child.

This she maintained throughout her appearance in the magistrate's court, and her subsequent trial. But she refused to name the real mother. She refused to name anyone who knew her or had even seen her. She refused to explain why her own name was on the boy's birth certificate, found in her possession, and checked with the Registrar's entry.

'What could her legal advisers do?' Frances asked her two visitors, who sat staring at her as she finished her story, too subdued by the grim tale to say anything at all. 'How could anyone help her, when she refused to help them? They suggested she should plead insanity, but she refused, and the doctors who saw her said they could not support such a plea. Besides, what she said was not true. I *knew* it wasn't true. The part about the child not being hers. I was there.'

'You were actually present when the baby was born?'

'Well, no. I was on a job, as I told you. They – they sent me to another factory on a special training course, for a few weeks, and when I came back the baby was there and Helen was looking after it.'

'She was in bed?'

'Actually she was up. It was just over a week old.'

'Was she feeding the child herself?' Mavis asked.

'No. Bottles,' said Frances, with a face of slight disgust.

'Then there was a chance she was speaking the truth?' said Reg. 'Or were there witnesses of the birth?'

'The prosecution didn't bring any. They considered it proved by the birth certificate and the landlady where she lived later on. The defence didn't bring any to prove the boy was not hers. I couldn't help. I *knew* she had been pregnant, and the dates corresponded, and all that.'

'You had to give that evidence?'

'Well, yes. I was on oath. The cross-examination was ghastly.'

Mrs Meadows covered her eyes with her hand as if the memory of the trial was still vivid in her mind, even after sixteen years.

'Why *should* she want to kill it, after three years?' Reg said, slowly. 'That's what I can't understand. They do it at once, sometimes, I know. But after all that time?'

'A fit of sudden rage,' suggested Frances. 'Don't think we haven't wondered and wondered ourselves, Colin and I. A sudden feeling that it was all too much for her.'

'Unmarried mothers are often unstable,' Mavis said. 'But it doesn't fit with Miss Trubb. What I can't see is her being an unmarried mother at all. I don't mean she'd be too unattractive. That photo they reproduced of her at the time of the trial . . . I mean to say, she was quite pretty then, if you allow for the clothes and hair style. A lovely figure, you'd say. But her character – '

'That's it,' Reg said. 'Character. It's a proper mystery, isn't it, Mrs Meadows? Was there an appeal?'

'Oh, yes. That was before the reprieve. There was a big petition. It was wonderful how many people were against the execution.'

'That's Joy!' Mavis interrupted, suddenly, jumping up from her chair. 'I'm sure I heard her.'

None of them could see the car from the depths of their comfortable chairs. Reg and Mrs Meadows followed Mavis to the window.

'She must have woken up,' said Frances, kindly. 'Won't you bring her in?'

They all went out into the drive. Joy was screaming loudly and thrashing about in her carry-cot.

'Looks like something's frightened her,' Mavis said, leaning into the car to pick up the baby. 'She's very sensitive to strangers.'

'But there is no one here,' said Mrs Meadows, rather white in the face. 'Colin went off to play golf, as usual, and my help doesn't come on Sunday. There is no one here except myself.'

'Anyone could come up the drive,' said Reg. 'The gate is open.'

'We would have heard footsteps on the gravel,' said Mavis, 'with the window open as it was. I heard Joy directly.'

The Holmeses decided not to go in again, but to leave at once. Joy would settle down again when the car was moving, Mavis said. They refused an invitation to tea.

'Well, if you must go,' Frances said, holding out her hand with a charming smile. 'Colin will be disappointed to have missed you.'

'Thank you,' Mavis answered. 'And for all you've told us. I know it will set our minds at rest.'

'I don't know so much about that,' Reg said. 'I think it ought to be gone into again. I think she ought to speak up, even now. I'd like to tell her so. If she won't, I think someone ought to go into the real origin of that child she's supposed to have murdered. As I said to Mavis, and I say it again, our Miss Trubb isn't the type to murder anyone, least of all a little child.'

CHAPTER 5

Miss Trubb sat in the Ladies' Room at Weyford Station. She was waiting for the train that would take her back to London. She felt very tired, because she had walked fast through the back streets of the town. Giddy, too, and rather faint. She knew she had not yet fully recovered from her harrowing experience.

She was very near to tears. It was the first time she had visited Weyford for more than eighteen years, and she found the place much changed, with large new Council estates stretching across land she had known as open country, dotted with small farms. Unproductive farms, she remembered her father saying very often. Poor chalky land, mopping up the gratuities of the First War veterans, breaking their hearts as the fighting had broken their bodies. The farms were of little value. So what did it matter that they had gone? Only another reminder of the great waste in her life, the huge gap that could never be filled.

It was not only the growth of the town that had upset her. Familiar shops had changed hands, grown new fronts, wide impersonal glass expanses in place of the individual small showcases developed from the front windows of small dignified eighteenth-century town houses. She had not dared to pass by her own former home, so she had not suffered the sharpest pang of all in finding it gone, demolished after her father's death, very profitably for Frances and Colin, to make way for a modern block of flats. But she had meant to see Frances, to appeal to her for the last time for help, for relief from fear.

It would have to be the last time. She could not go on any longer, harried by this constant fear. She had nothing to lose, so why did she fight? Why not let that ultimate fate, so long dreaded, so long brooded upon, sweep over her, blotting out her useless, painful existence? Why not?

A woman came out of the inner part of the Ladies' Waiting Room, looking about her with a cross anxious face.

'Have you seen my little boy?' she asked Miss Trubb, abruptly.

The latter stared at her, trying to take in what she had said.

'Little boy?' she asked, with the old familiar pang of envy.

'Yes. I told him to wait till I came out.'

'There was no one here when I came in. No one at all,' said Miss Trubb, slowly.

The woman made an impatient sound.

'Children!' she snapped, making for the door. 'More trouble than they're worth!'

She was gone, the door banging shut behind her.

'No,' Miss Trubb told herself, thinking now of Joy Holmes, 'always worth it. Always.'

She was led back to her former thoughts. Frances had a nice place now; a bit overgrown, with all those bushes in the drive, but where would she have been without them? She smiled a little as she thought of herself dodging so quickly behind a laurel bush when she caught sight of the Holmes's car. She would have stayed hidden till they left, in the hope of seeing Frances later. If only Joy had not been frightened when –

Miss Trubb looked at her watch. Still another quarter of an hour to wait for the fast train. She had just missed the slow one. She leaned back and shut her eyes, drifting away into a confusion of images, half dreamed, half remembered. Until a childish voice brought her to herself with words that struck at her heart.

'I want my mummy.'

A small boy, about four years old, stood just inside the door of the Waiting Room, looking about with an air of arrogance assumed to cover his growing panic.

Miss Trubb understood at once.

'She told you to wait here for her, didn't she?'

'I was.'

'You weren't here when I came in. And your mummy was inside, then. She asked me where you had gone.'

His face closed up. He was not going to tell *anyone*.

'She has gone out to look for you. But I expect she'll come back here. You had better stay with me.'

The child still stood by the door, sullen, afraid, but determined never to acknowledge his fault.

'Come and sit down,' said Miss Trubb, smiling, 'and I'll tell you a story till Mummy comes for you.'

Without a word the boy turned and, dragging the heavy door open a little, struggled through and was gone.

Miss Trubb jumped up, all her deep depression swept away by her anxiety for the child. He was naughty, disobedient, as unprepossessing as his mother, from whom doubtless he had learned these ways. But he was too young to be allowed to roam at large on a railway station. Someone must look after him.

She ran out on to the platform, and seeing the small figure not far away, hurried towards him.

It was unfortunate that the boy's mother, returning distracted now towards the Waiting Room, should catch sight of her child at the moment he caught sight of the pursuing Miss Trubb. The boy began to run, Miss Trubb broke into a lumbering trot. He caught sight of his mother just ahead, her furious face promising all he feared. Trapped between two avenging adults, he swerved, running blindly towards the edge of the platform, just as the fast train for London began to draw into it.

Miss Trubb reached for him wildly and narrowly missed falling on the line herself. The child was seized and firmly held by a porter. The mother screamed. The train came to a stop with a rattling of door handles as the carriages opened.

'Yours, is he?' said the porter, impassive, pushing the boy towards the younger of the two panting women. 'Not safe to let them career about a station like that.'

'I didn't. He went off on his own.' She shook her child by the arm until he began to cry. 'It was that woman frightened him.'

'What woman?' The porter was mystified.

'She ran after me,' whimpered the child, seeing a loophole for himself. 'She was there. She followed me.'

'That's right,' said the woman. 'She was. I saw her. She might have thrown him under the train, if you hadn't caught hold of him.'

The porter turned away, anxious to leave the hysterical pair. They were not his business, anyhow.

But Miss Trubb, leaning against a station luggage trolley, fighting for breath, heard what the mother said, and her knees grew weak with fear. She managed to turn her back on the platform and the train, until she remembered that it must be the one she was waiting for. With an enormous effort, she moved towards it and climbed into a carriage, sat down on the further side, and turned her head to look out of the window.

The mother of the boy stared about her for some time, trying to see Miss Trubb. She wanted desperately to give her a piece of her mind for endangering the life of her little boy. But the convenient scapegoat was nowhere to be seen. Sneaked off, like a criminal. Like a criminal, she said later, when she retold this story to her friends. She repeated it many times in the next week or two. And many of them said that there were some queer characters about these days, and you couldn't be too careful. Mad or wicked, or both. Look at that ex-convict, that Miss Trubb, who had tried to gas herself. Good job if she'd brought it off, but no, they had to resuscitate her, and what would *she* be up to next?

Reg Holmes was far from satisfied by his interview with Mrs Meadows. As he explained to Mavis on the drive home, there were several very queer features in the case. The medical side, for instance. If Miss Trubb, as she swore on oath, had not had a child at all, why was no doctor called to support her plea? Surely they could tell? Mavis was not sure.

'I know what I'll do,' Reg said. 'I'll get hold of the old numbers of one of the papers that report trials verbatim, near enough. *The Times* would be the one, wouldn't it?'

'I don't know,' said Mavis. 'There used to be a copy at the place where I worked with Carol, in the clients' waiting-room, but I can't say I ever opened it. Too long and too dry, by half.'

They laughed.

'All the same,' Reg went on, 'it'll be our best bet for a start. I know, because our firm had an action a couple of years back and I read it up to see who was in the wrong.'

'It was the other side, I suppose?'

'Well, what d'you think? I'm still with the same firm.'

Mavis gave her husband an admiring glance. He had such a clear head. He thought of everything. Watching his strong hands on the wheel of the car, and his steady gaze at the road ahead, she gave a little sigh of content for his love and protection. He'd never let them down, herself and Joy. So if he was interested in poor old Miss Trubb. . . .

'You go ahead, darling,' she said, indulgently. 'I don't know that you'll get anywhere, after all this time. But there's no harm in satisfying your mind, is there?'

Reg went about it with his usual quiet energy, and by Wednesday evening had made a survey of all the newspaper material he could come by. It left him no less curious, and very far from satisfied.

'There are a lot of absolutely obvious snags,' he said, 'to finding her guilty. It must have been largely prejudice. There were three women on the jury. You'd get a big sentimental bias against her, there.'

'Don't be so cold-blooded!'

'I'm not. But it's a fact. Women would naturally take the emotional view, and the men wouldn't like to go against them, for fear of being thought unrespectable or callous, like you did.'

'All right. What are the obvious snags?'

'I'm going to write to the barrister in the case,' said Reg, not answering her directly.

'He won't take any notice. You might have more chance with the solicitor. They see them first, don't they?'

It was Reg's turn to admire.

'You do study cases, then?'

Mavis made a face at him.

'No, I don't. But there was that radio series about the law. It said about solicitors.'

'Right. I've got all the names. I'll write tonight.'

Though she agreed with Reg's plans, and applauded the interest he was taking in Miss Trubb, Mavis had really begun to lose interest in the case. It had happened so long ago. How could you find out things now, when no one had been able to find them out before? Besides, Mrs Meadows was sure there had been no mistake, and though she had been only a girl at the time, no one in the late thirties had been so innocent or ignorant as to make a mistake about whether her own sister was pregnant or not. It was impossible.

Mrs Meadows was still sorry about it all. You could tell that from the way she spoke. She had been most reluctant to put any blame on Miss Trubb for anything she had done. Well then, if nice Mrs Meadows took that line, what were they worrying about? Of course Reg must satisfy himself. He was not one to leave anything in the air. She would listen and encourage him, until he got tired of it. But personally. . . .

The shops were very crowded on Friday morning. Mavis pushed Joy's pram hard up against the outside of the grocer's, and put the brake on. It really wasn't fair, she thought, to take the pram inside, bumping against everyone's legs. Besides, it was better for Joy to be in the open air, away from other people's germs. The polio epidemic that year was still going on. Much safer outside. She smoothed the cover of the pram over the sleeping child and went into the shop.

The queues at the counters were long, and Mavis had the week-end groceries to buy. The whole proceeding took her nearly half an hour. But she left the shop with two filled shopping bags, and nothing left to get but the fresh fruit. She had already visited her butcher; the Sunday joint would be delivered in the morning.

Joy was still asleep, Mavis saw, as she threaded her way through the crowd in the doorway of the shop. But she also saw, with annoyance, as she drew nearer, that some litter-minded person had dropped a piece of paper on to the clean embroidered cover of the pram. She put both shoppings bags into one hand and swept at the offending paper with the other. It did not move. It was pinned in place. It was a grubby single sheet of writing paper, folded across. It was addressed in pencilled printed capitals to MRS. HOLMES.

Mavis's heart jerked and raced on. But she put her bags down on the pavement very quietly and unpinned the note, taking the greatest care not to disturb Joy. Leaning against the shop window, because she had begun to feel weak and cold, she read, 'This is a warning. If you do not stop meddling in affairs that don't concern you, your child will suffer. This is not a joke.'

It was not, indeed. Even if it were a hoax, a perverted elaborate trick on the part of some near-lunatic, it was too cruel, too callous, to be a joke. Mavis shut her eyes, not able to bear the sight of those crudely printed words. But the paper was still in her hand, and a voice at her side said kindly, 'Are you all right?'

Mavis opened her eyes and looked round. An elderly woman was staring at her, anxiously. She forced herself to smile.

'Yes, thank you. It – it was very hot inside the shop.'

'Too much of a rush these days,' the woman said. 'I don't know how you young mothers manage. I don't, really.'

Mavis smiled again. The woman helped her to load her shopping into the end of the pram, and walked at her side to the next cross-roads. There their ways separated, and Mavis went home. She took Joy's pram indoors, and for the rest of that day kept the child beside her.

When Reg saw the note he was first appalled, then furious, then deeply thoughtful.

'Someone's got the wind up,' he said, at last. 'Doesn't want us to open up the case again. Who can that be, do you think? The Meadows couple are the only ones that even know we're interested.'

'What about the solicitors you wrote to, Monday?'

'Are you suggesting they threatened Joy?'

'Not, of course not. But they'd be able to get in touch with anyone in the case. What exactly did they say in their letter back? Wasn't it something to do with consulting people?'

Reg got out the letter, which had come by return of post.

'It says they appreciate our interest in the case in view of recent events. That means the so-called suicide attempt. But they cannot undertake to give us any information without consulting various persons originally concerned. I suppose that's some of the witnesses at the trial. The defence witnesses.'

'Why should one of them want to stop us?'

'God knows. If they do. The obvious people to stop us are the Meadows couple. Not wanting to revive something it must have taken them years to live down.'

'But they'd just write and ask us to stop, out of consideration for their feelings, or something like that. They wouldn't come all the way from Weyford to pin a crazy note on Joy's pram cover.'

'It doesn't fit with Mrs Meadows, certainly. But it couldn't have been Miss Trubb herself, could it? She didn't know we were going to Weyford.'

'Is she still at the hospital?'

'I don't know. I haven't inquired this week. Have you?'

'No.' Mavis looked ashamed. 'Don't you think it's awful of us to be taking all this trouble on her behalf, and not even to ring up and ask how she is?'

Reg did not answer. He got up and went out into the hall to telephone. But he heard Mavis's voice, continuing, 'We're only doing it out of sheer darned curiosity, aren't we? I think we ought to lay off, like the note says.'

When Reg went back into the sitting-room he was looking very grave.

'Don't say she's had a relapse!' Mavis exclaimed.

'No. She's well. So well, they discharged her last Saturday. She said she wanted to go, they couldn't keep her on medical grounds, and the police were not going to bring a charge. So she left. She may be anywhere.'

'She could have gone to Weyford on Sunday, then,' Mavis said, her face whitening. 'She could have put two and two together and written that note.'

'If she doesn't want us to find out more about her, it must mean she was guilty after all.'

'I think it means she's crazy.'

But Reg was obstinate.

'She never was crazy. But it could mean she didn't clear

47

herself in the first place, because she was shielding someone else. And she wants us to stop now for the same reason.'

'But could she threaten Joy if she isn't mad?'

'I don't know.' Reg made up his mind. 'There's one thing I ought to do. Show the note to the police. If they take it up, we can drop out. Might be best all round if we did.'

Mavis agreed. She also proposed to ask her mother, a widow, to pay them a visit for a week or two, to help her keep watch over Joy. Reg thought her fears excessive, but was not unwilling to take extra precautions.

His visit to the police was disappointing. Inspector Brown inclined to the hoax theory. Alternatively, he thought it proved Miss Trubb was mental, and getting more so. Probably she'd turn up on a railway line, or in the river, and that would set all their minds at rest.

Reg was indignant. It was the duty of the police to follow up this clue. If Miss Trubb had not written the note, and they were the people to prove this, then who did? The answer might solve the riddle of sixteen years ago, which was never satisfactorily solved.

But Inspector Brown would not move. Sixteen years ago they had got a conviction, even if the sentence was upset by the Home Secretary of the day. They had no wish to upset the results of the Conington police of that time. The note was a hoax. It was impossible to find the joker. Miss Trubb was almost certainly mad. She always had been mad. She ought to have pleaded insanity when she knocked off her little boy. The jury would have agreed to that. If it hadn't been for the local magistrate this time, she would have been certified a week ago. The doctors were nearly always for it, but the magistrates were very cagey, always afraid the relations and friends, and the doctors, even, wanted to get rid of a nuisance, for their own sakes. Half the time, it was true, of course.

Reg grew impatient of this lumbering cynicism. He took back the note and put it away in his wallet.

'If anything happens to Joy,' he said, 'you can't say I haven't warned you.'

Brown watched him go with impassive eyes. He was not impressed. It happened like this so often.

CHAPTER 6

Claud Warrington-Reeve, Q.C., had chambers in one of the Inns of Court. From his window he looked out at tall trees shading smooth lawns. On this October morning the leaves were falling, making golden pools on the grass round each dark trunk. Mr Warrington-Reeve looked at the scene with approval while he waited for his clerk to bring in his visitor.

So Reg, entering the room, saw only the back of a grey head, set on a short heavy neck. A second later, however, he was disconcerted by a pair of surprisingly bright dark eyes turned on him with frank inquiry.

'Mr Holmes, sir,' said the clerk, and retreated at once.

'I hope – ' began Reg, beginning his prepared apology.

'Sit down.'

Warrington-Reeve did not get up, but his voice was friendly. The order was an invitation, however ungraciously expressed. Reg sat down, interested and not at all resentful.

'It's good of you to see me, sir,' he began. 'Mr Coke said – '

'Yes.' The interruption was again without offence. 'Mr Coke no doubt told you he was not with the firm when this case was tried. Nor was Mr Frank Simmonds. And *his* father retired several years ago.'

'Yes, sir. That was pretty much what he said. He didn't give me much hopes of being able to see you, which is why – '

'Exactly. But you see, I am interested myself. And though I may as well tell you at the start I very seriously thought of throwing up the brief when Miss Trubb refused to plead insanity, by the end of it I did realize that plea would not have been supported by the evidence.'

Reg looked relieved.

'That's what we think,' he exclaimed. 'I mean, Mavis and I. She's my wife. All this poppycock in the papers – '

'Quite. Quite. I have read the papers, Mr Holmes. I was interested when she turned up again, as I said before. Now, I have not much time. Tell me, as briefly as you can, and as directly, what exactly you want from me.'

'I don't think she tried to commit suicide,' Reg said firmly, 'far less tried to harm me and my family. I think someone else is responsible. And you see what that means, don't you, sir?'

It was clear, from the sudden gleam in those dark eyes, that Mr Warrington-Reeve saw the whole situation and many of its implications.

'Are you trying to suggest that some ill-intentioned person has deliberately tried to do away with Miss Trubb and possibly you and your family at the same time? That having failed, in such a way as to arouse your curiosity, that person is now trying to frighten you in order to stop your inquiries? Do you read detective stories, Mr Holmes?'

Reg blushed. This was the first offensive thing the eminent counsel had said, and for a few seconds Reg saw himself in court being cross-questioned in these blandly cutting terms, and understood why Mr Reeve had reached his present pinnacle. It was not so much the actual words he used, but the way he spoke. Was that their gimmick? Was that how they all acted?

'No, I don't,' he answered. 'But if you'll let me, I'll give you my reasons for thinking as I do.'

Warrington-Reeve began to respect the young man. He was capable of concentration, of laying aside his feelings in order to put his case. Here was the stuff of a first-class witness.

'Go on,' he said, simply, and drawing a sheet of paper towards him, took up the gold-handled pencil on his table.

'First the kitchen window,' said Reg, and broke off to ask, anxiously. 'Mr Coke did give you the outline of the story, sir, didn't he?'

'He did, and I have read it carefully.'

'Well, then. The first time we went back, to fetch Joy away, and smelled gas, and I went into the kitchen, and the taps were off, the window was shut, because I opened it. I left it open. The next morning, when the house was full of gas, the window was shut, because we broke it from the outside.'

'Miss Trubb would naturally shut it if she wanted to gas herself.'

'Agreed. And stop up the ventilator, too. From the inside you'd think. But the ventilator was plugged on the *outside*. With moss. To look as if it had fallen there by accident. Moss! I ask you! My roof's practically new.'

And he was justly proud of it, the barrister saw, and smiled.

'Then where did the moss come from?'

'The lawn, possibly. There's a lot there, I'm afraid.'

'In other words it must have been put there deliberately, and rather stupidly?'

'Agreed,' Reg went on. 'So, if someone from outside had wanted to get in, they could have done so after we left, without her knowing. I didn't tell her I'd opened the window.'

The barrister nodded.

'And another thing. If it was suicide, why didn't she stay in the kitchen, and get the full benefit? They mostly do. Why go away upstairs, even if she shut all the windows?'

'The general conclusion this time has been mental instability. But go on.'

'The question of the rent she owed us. She didn't leave it for us at the time, but she sent it on, later. She was always very considerate. If she was going for good, you'd have thought she would settle up first. I don't think she was going for good. Not out of this world. I think she was leaving *us*, but not suicide.'

'Have you any other evidence to support that?'

'Yes. When we went in to fetch Joy, she was up and dressed, Miss Trubb, I mean, with the light off in her room. I think she wanted us to believe she'd gone to bed, and then she was going to creep off unbeknown to us. She had a pencil in her hand when she came to her door. I think she'd been writing her note when she heard us coming, earlier than she expected. And she never finished properly.'

'How do you mean?'

'That letter to her sister. It wasn't sealed and stamped. That's not like Miss Trubb. She's a trained secretary. And the paper had wavy edges, cut edges, not pulled ones, like fancy paper usually is. The line that ended "going away" had a dip just there. I think she may have put where she was going, and someone cut it off to make it seem like a suicide note.'

'Are you sure you don't read ...' the barrister began, smiling. 'Or perhaps you are a descendant of Sherlock, the immortal?' He broke off, seeing a heavy frown beginning to gather on Reg's face. 'It is a fanciful theory,' he said, in an altered voice. 'But stranger things have been done. It certainly impressed me as curious that the note should have been put in your brief-case. It would have been more usual to leave it at the bedside – to be found at once.'

'Playing for time,' said Reg.

'Who? Miss Trubb? Or the hypothetical villain who is gunning for her?'

Reg got up. It was no use. This clever chap, with his heavy sarcasm, was not going to help.

'Sit down,' said Warrington-Reeve again, and this time it was an order, meant to be obeyed. Reg sat down.

'You have not finished. Please do so. And you must be prepared to have your views attacked, even torn to shreds, and still be capable of defending them. Don't you understand what you are doing? You are trying to accuse some person or persons unknown of a criminal action. Indirectly you are trying to upset a verdict found in a court of law, and upheld on appeal. That is a very serious thing. You don't expect me to agree with everything you say on a first hearing, do you?'

'There was a doubt,' said Reg, stubbornly, 'at the time. There must have been, for the Home Secretary to grant a reprieve.'

'The doubts in the minds of humane politicians have very little to do with evidence, when it comes to a legal killing,' said Warrington-Reeve. 'I am telling you about the law, which is necessarily difficult and complicated.'

'There was just one other thing,' said Reg, subdued, but still obstinate. 'It looks on the face of it as if Miss Trubb went to Weyford the Sunday we did, to warn us off, perhaps even to stop us seeing her sister and getting the story of her past. You could make something of the fact that Joy was disturbed and started yelling. But Mavis and I don't agree that it was Miss Trubb. Joy yells at complete strangers but she always took to Miss Trubb. From the very start. If she woke her up, Joy wouldn't mind, she'd be pleased.'

'That is hardly evidence,' murmured the barrister.

There was silence in the room. Reg wanted to go, but dared not move. Mr Warrington-Reeve had turned his head away, and seemed to be staring at the golden leaf pools on the grass at the other side of the quiet lawn. The traffic was a faint murmur only, in this book-lined room. The rooks, high in the trees, made more noise.

At last the barrister turned his head.

'You have brought me your new evidence, if it can be called that,' he said. 'Have you anything to ask me on the subject of the old evidence, the evidence at the trial?'

'Yes, sir, please. Several things.'

'Mr Coke tells me you have informed yourself of the trial in great detail, as far as the newspapers reported it. So go ahead. I can tell you no more than what was actually said at the time. But I may be able to make it clearer.'

'Well, first of all, sir, the evidence of the birth of the child. Miss Trubb said it wasn't hers, but she refused to say whose it was. Now, why couldn't it be proved in her favour? I mean to say, if she didn't have a child, couldn't you bring medical evidence to say she didn't?'

'It ought to have been simple. It was not. She was not attended by a doctor, but by a midwife.'

'She?'

'The mother of the child, shall we say? That midwife, a district nurse, was not available to us. She had gone abroad and could not be traced. Remember, it was war-time.'

'I'd have thought that would make it easier. You couldn't go abroad without its being known.'

The barrister smiled.

'You have a refreshingly clear mind,' he said. 'Yes, you are right. This nurse joined an Army Nursing Unit, was transferred to an Army hospital in Scotland, and from there to

Canada, where she married a Canadian, left the Forces, and at the time of the trial she could not be traced.'

'I see. Well then, couldn't you prove Miss Trubb didn't have a baby?'

'We tried that. She submitted herself to an examination by a consultant gynaecologist. She hoped this would prove her claim. But his report said that owing to an operation of a minor type performed in her late teens for a mild gynaecological disorder, it was not possible to say definitely that she had *not* had a child, though there was no definite evidence, in the shape of scars and so on, to show that she *had*. Apparently many women emerge from a first pregnancy and childbirth without a blemish.'

'That's right,' said Reg, thinking of Mavis's smooth stomach and firm breasts, and immediately blushing as he saw the barrister quietly weighing his thoughts.

'Well, what about the landlady?' he hurried on, anxious to change the subject.

'Another misfortune for us. The landlady and her house were bombed, while Miss Trubb and the child were in it. They escaped unhurt, but the landlady was killed and the house practically demolished.'

'So you never found anyone who could say that Miss Trubb actually had that baby herself?'

'No. The nearest to it was her sister, who, after all, did give evidence of Miss Trubb's pregnancy.'

'Based on what?'

'On her observation and on what she said Miss Trubb told her.'

'Did Miss Trubb confirm or deny Mrs Meadows's evidence?'

'She refused to discuss it. Beyond denying that she could ever have told her sister in so many words that she was pregnant, because she was never in that condition.'

'What did Mrs Meadows have to say to that?'

'She agreed that the actual words were not spoken between them, but she asserted that they did not have to be. Helen's behaviour told her all she needed to know.'

'Behaviour? Not her appearance?'

'We naturally pressed her on that. She did not actually see her sister, she said, during the last few weeks.'

'I suppose you checked that?'

'There was no way of doing so. Miss Trubb did not deny it. With the landlady gone, there was no one to ask. All the same it is usually possible to decide more than a few weeks before the birth.'

'It certainly is. What about the factory where Miss Trubb worked?'

'She had stopped attending there. And also she was drawing extra rations, and the rest of the stuff they gave them at the Food Office.'

'It does look bad, doesn't it?' Reg said, coming to the end of his suggestions.

'It always looked extremely bad.'

'All the same,' Reg went on, as a new thought came to him. 'It could have been the other way round.'

'How do you mean?'

'How about Mrs Meadows being the one that had the baby?'

The barrister sighed.

'Naturally we thought of that when Miss Trubb insisted she was looking after someone else's child. It seemed impossible she would make such a sacrifice of her reputation and whole way of living unless it was for someone she was particularly devoted to. But we were in the same quandary over this. Mrs Meadows quite willingly gave us particulars of where she had been and they were verified as far as possible. In some cases it was not possible. There was great confusion in 1940, you may remember.'

'I don't,' said Reg. 'Not to be that much impressed by it.'

'No, I suppose not.' Warrington-Reeve smiled, with quite human warmth. 'Well, there was.'

'You could have tried to find out if Mrs Meadows had had a baby,' suggested Reg.

'Oh, she had. By her husband, Colin Meadows. Miss Trubb's child was three years old when he was murdered. Mrs Meadows had been married over two years and her own first child was nearly a year old at the time of the trial.'

This was the last straw, Reg decided, and said so. The barrister agreed with him.

'We did our best,' he said. 'But, as you see, we were brought up against blank walls in every direction. Moreover, and this was one of the prosecution's main arguments, there was no denying Miss Trubb was looking after the boy at the time of his death. Whether he was her child or not, he was living with her and was found dead in his cot in the room next to hers at her lodgings. Whether he was her child or not, apparently she had killed him. She was alone in the house at the time.'

'Yes, I see what you mean,' Reg said, in a very low voice.

He thanked Mr Warrington-Reeve and got up to go. The latter went with him to the door. Reg turned awkwardly.

'I'm sorry to have taken up so much of your time,' he said. 'Mr Coke said your fee – '

The barrister laid his hand for a moment on the young man's shoulder.

'Never mind my fee,' he said, cheerfully. 'We'll talk about that if this leads anywhere. I've always felt I ought in some way to have managed Miss Trubb's case better. On the face of it, it was hopeless. And then, of course, the poor woman had little or no money. Mrs Meadows offered to pay for any investigation we wanted to make, but Miss Trubb forbade us to take that offer. Really her attitude was, "I didn't do it. I can't prove I didn't. You can't prove I did. Let matters take their course." Which, naturally, they did, in the obvious direction.'

'All the same – ' Reg began.

'All the same, you intend to go on with what you've begun, don't you? In view of what you've told me, I think you ought to be careful. I'll have a word with one of the Scotland Yard chaps. It wasn't in their hands before. The local people at Conington looked after it. But they ought to hear about that note your wife got.'

'Inspector Brown turned it down as a hoax.'

'Yes, I know. But if it wasn't, it might mean, only *might*, mind you, that someone very carefully hidden for sixteen years is beginning to show himself. And that, with all proper precautions, should be encouraged.'

'Do you really think so?' Reg's spirits began to take an upward curve.

'Yes, I do. If anything else comes your way, I want to hear of it at once, please. So we'll cut the question of fees at present, since it is not clear which of us is employing the other.'

On this cordial note they shook hands and parted.

Mr Coke was interested to hear Reg's report of his interview with counsel, and gratified by the latter's behaviour. The letter in which he expressed all this was much less formal than before, and he enclosed, on Reg's request, the address of the landlady in Conington at whose former house the murder had taken place. Reg lost no time in following this up. On the next Sunday, leaving Joy in charge of her grandmother, he and Mavis got up early and drove to the big Midlands town.

They found the house without too much difficulty. It was in a respectable but not wealthy district, and stood up in solid Victorian grey stone among a cluster of small new dwellings. But the whole town, having been extensively bombed in the war, had a patchwork appearance. The new houses, and many still being built, had not had time to mellow and take their natural place with the old. That place had been prepared in an altogether too unnatural fashion.

Mrs Ogden was at home. In fact their way was made easy for them by the notice on her gate which said, 'Guest House. Non-residents catered for'. They went in and ordered lunch, and being the only strangers present were regarded with a good deal of curiosity by the residents.

After the meal Mavis asked to speak to Mrs Ogden. She and Reg were led to a room marked 'Office', and left there. Mrs Ogden, pleasant and friendly, with very curled white hair, joined them almost at once.

If she was disappointed that this nice young couple did not want to book the vacant double room, she did not show it. But when they explained the reason for their visit, her face tightened.

'What do you want to know for?' she asked. 'Not another

famous trial series, I hope? I've had enough of that sort of thing from the Press and the radio all these years.'

They assured her that they had nothing to do with either, but were would-be champions of Miss Trubb.

Mrs Ogden needed further enlightenment. She had missed the paragraph about the poor woman. After all these years! What a dreadful thing! And so soon after her release.

'I'm sure you remember the time of the little boy's death,' said Mavis.

'Could I ever forget it? Nor that poor soul, shaking and sobbing, and fainting. I thought she'd die or go out of her mind.'

'Did you think she'd done it?' Reg asked, bluntly.

'I didn't know what to think. You see, she could have. She was alone in the house that night. Not this house, you understand; we left that one after the trial, for business reasons.'

'Yes. Mr Coke, who was Miss Trubb's solicitor then, gave me your new address. He said he thought you would be able to help us, or at any rate would speak to us about it.'

Mrs Ogden nodded.

'He wrote for my permission,' she said. 'I'm always willing to give any help if I can. I didn't realize it would be you two. I envisaged old friends of hers.'

'Why was she alone in the house?' Mavis asked.

'Because it so happened I had no other guests just then. Though actually we had an inquiry from a convalescent officer that morning. War-time, you understand. People came and went. Sometimes I'd be so full I didn't know how to turn round, and then for a couple of days I'd not have a soul.'

'Why was she alone?' Reg insisted.

'I'd gone to my sister's because she was down with flu –'

'Just like it happened to us,' Mavis interrupted, excitedly. 'We were away at a friend's, who was taken suddenly ill. At least, we were going to be away.'

'But we went back to tell Miss Trubb, and to get our little girl,' Reg explained, more lucidly.

'Still, I do see the resemblance,' Mrs Ogden agreed. 'It might have crossed her mind, too, after you'd gone, and she couldn't stand the memory.'

'That part of the town you were in then, was it more central than this?' asked Reg. 'I mean to say, would there be more people about outside in the normal way?'

'A fair number. It was near a recreation ground. You got mothers with children and old people who liked to go in and sit on the seats. Surprising how many of them there were considering the bombing. But people got used to it, and a lot refused to be evacuated. Then there were the convalescents from the hospital out at Mayfield. War wounded. They were hanging about in their blue suits all day long. But they had to be out of the town by nightfall.'

'So it wouldn't have been easy for a suspicious character to watch your house?'

'Well, it would and it wouldn't. He'd be lost in a crowd so to speak, but the soldier boys would be likely to spot him. They had nothing to do but loaf about.'

'Quite. I just wondered if the murder wasn't a plain case of burglary? Burglar got in, having watched you go off, the baby whimpered, and he put the pillow over its face to stop the noise.'

'That was the only suggestion her counsel made, wasn't it?'

'Yes.'

'They never found anyone who saw a suspicious character near my house that evening, or any other time.'

'When did you get back?' asked Reg, trying to return to definite facts.

'About ten in the morning. The police had been called then. You see, she said all along, as I was away, she'd taken the liberty of putting little Tom in the small bedroom next to hers, because she had a bad cold coming on, and didn't want him to catch it. She went in to him before she went to bed herself, and he was sleeping naturally. She took some aspirin and codeine that night for her cold and slept heavily. She went in again in the morning, and he was lying there with the pillow over his face, dead.'

'Little children oughtn't to have pillows,' said Mavis. 'Not before they're four.'

'Tom was over three, and a big boy. It was no accident, though, as the doctor saw straightaway when she called him.'

'Miss Trubb sent for the doctor?'

'At once. She was nearly out of her mind, but she had the sense to do that. It was when he told her it had been done deliberately, between midnight and four in the morning, that she collapsed. He sent for the ambulance, the doctor did, and for the police. So I never saw the poor little fellow. Just as well, I expect. Only her. They took her away the same day. She was in the prison hospital for weeks. I wouldn't have known her at the trial.'

'You gave evidence, didn't you?'

'Just the date she came to me, which was November 4th in '42. I remember the date, because the weather was getting foggy, and she showed me a few little fireworks she'd bought for next day, to let off for Tom, and she said she hoped it would be clear so he could enjoy them, and that I wouldn't mind if she used my back garden. That was a year before he died, poor lamb. She was always quiet, you see, but jolly underneath, as far as the boy was concerned.'

'Did you know where she'd come from?'

'Another part of the town. Before that she'd been bombed out of her first digs. Lucky to be alive. It was the billeting officer sent her to me, knowing I'd a vacancy at the time for a war worker.'

'Was no one left in her first lodgings to give evidence about the child's birth?'

'Not a soul, as far as I know. They dug her out, her and little Tom.'

'You liked her, didn't you?' Mavis asked.

Mrs Ogden nodded.

'Up to the time they brought her in guilty.'

'You didn't think she'd killed the child?'

'I couldn't believe it, till then. She thought the world of him,' said Mrs Ogden. 'I've never seen a more devoted mother. Unusual, too. They don't like them as a rule.'

Reg nodded. He knew what she meant. It was one of the reasons he wanted to get to the bottom of this. He said so to Mavis as they drove away from Mrs Ogden's house.

'Bastards don't often get the affection Miss Trubb showed,' he said. 'Which makes me wonder all the more, was he really her child, or wasn't he?'

CHAPTER 7

It was still early in the afternoon when the Holmeses left Mrs Ogden's guest house. She went down to the road with them to see them into their car.

'Beaconsfield Road, about half-way along on the right hand side. There's a board outside, over the clinic entrance. You can't miss it.'

Reg thanked her, Mavis waved good-bye and they drove away, leaving Mrs Ogden a little puzzled, and more than a little disturbed at the thought of further publicity. The former occasion had set her back for several years. Not during the later war-time rush for lodgings in a town manufacturing armaments, but after the war, when people remembered she had been mixed up with a murderess.

She watched the car until it turned the corner, and then, with a sigh for the heavy troubles of this world, went back into her house.

Reg found the headquarters of the District Nurses without difficulty. He and Mavis went in and were fortunate enough to find the Sister-in-Charge at home. Reg put the case to her. Practice was perfecting his story. He had reduced it to a few informative sentences. But he had doubts about the outcome in this case. The trim figure before him looked far too young to have been in authority sixteen years before. He was relieved, therefore, to find that she already knew of the case. She nodded and picked up a letter on her desk.

'I had this from a solicitor in Weyford, not long ago,' she said. 'A Mr Coke. Here it is. He says some people who are interested in Miss Trubb, having come in contact with her since her release, are making certain inquiries. You are the people he means, I suppose?'

'Yes, we are. What we want to know, Sister, is anything you can tell us about the birth of Miss Trubb's child, if it *was* her child. Not the medical side,' he hastened to add, seeing the usual professional blankness beginning to spread over the nurse's face. 'I know that's none of our business.'

'What Reg means is quite simple,' Mavis said. 'We can't believe the child was Miss Trubb's at all. At the trial she said it wasn't. There was no definite evidence that it was. I mean, the nurse who attended her was not there. No one was at the trial who could say, "That's the person who had the baby. I was there at the time, and saw it happen." '

'Yes,' Sister answered. 'I was not here then, myself, but I have looked out the records. You are lucky we still have them. Since the National Health Service started they make all sorts of sweeping regulations. One of them is that records of more than ten years' standing shall be destroyed. Our doctors were right up in arms against that, of course, and got it altered.'

'Why do they want to interfere with the doctors' records?'

'No space for storing them in the big hospitals, with all the extra apparatus for modern treatments, and the extra room needed for the administrative staff. Besides having no money to spare for building. I don't know. Perhaps just an idea in some official's mind, to put himself forward. You never know, do you?'

'That's right. Anyway, you had the records we want?'

'Yes, up to a point. I can tell you that a Miss Trubb, no initials given, had an illegitimate baby at her lodgings and it was a straightforward delivery. She did not attend the antenatal clinic, in spite of being told she must do so, or else we might not agree to attend her. It was a Nurse Walters who looked after her, but she left here soon afterwards.'

'Yes, we were told that. You never got her address in Canada?'

'No. She was quite out of touch with us long before she went abroad. The only address we had for her was her parents' home in the Lake District.'

Reg frowned.

'If you had that, why didn't Mr Coke get in touch with her through the parents?'

'I don't know, I'm afraid.'

'He told us,' Mavis said. 'Don't you remember? They lost touch with her when she left the Army Nursing Unit to get married to a Canadian.'

There was silence in the room for a few minutes. Then Reg broke it.

'You say she never turned up at the ante-natal clinic. I understand she did go to the Food Office to get the orange juice and that.'

'She had the extra ration book,' added Mavis.

Sister nodded.

'Didn't they get the Food Office people to identify her at the trial?' she asked.

'One of them gave evidence,' Reg answered. 'She said she recognized Miss Trubb as the lady who collected the doings. When Mr Warrington-Reeve, that was Miss Trubb's counsel, asked her if Miss Trubb was noticeably pregnant, she said she wouldn't like to swear to it, because the queues were very long and she worked very fast, handing out the stuff, and the counter was too high to see more than the head and shoulders of the customers, unless they were very tall. They had to suppress laughter in court at that crack. I read it in the papers.'

'I does seem difficult,' Sister said. 'What about the birth certificate? Surely that proves whose child it was?'

'It ought to,' Reg agreed. 'It's made out with the name of Helen Trubb as the mother, no name for the father. Her real name is Clements, but she never used it in Conington, and has kept to Trubb ever since, even after she came out.'

'How strange,' murmured Sister. 'To keep it, I mean. Our record has Clements in brackets, but no Christian name or initials, as I told you. I don't see how you can get round the birth certificate. Surely the Registrar could identify her as the mother of the child?'

'No. He was called up in 1941, joined the Pioneer Corps, and was killed in Egypt four months before the murder.'

'Well, really!' Sister exclaimed. 'There seems to have been

a positive plot to keep out anyone who could help one way or another.'

'Doesn't there?' said Mavis. 'That's what we feel. We were angry at first with Mr Coke, and the barrister, but were they up against it! They keep saying it was the war, and they're dead right, aren't they?'

But Sister was not attending. She felt that this inquiry was in some way a challenge to the efficiency of the organization she served. One of their midwives had delivered this woman, or else the woman she was shielding with such mad insistence. It ought not to be impossible to establish the truth. But how? The clinic was no good. The Food Office had failed. The Registrar's Office? In spite of the fact that the former man was no longer there? Or even his immediate successor?

'I've an idea,' she said. 'You could perhaps get the present Registrar to help you. He is very kind and not a bit official. My mothers always speak well of him. What I mean is, Miss Trubb can't have been the only one there in his office when she went down to register. Some of the others who came before or after her must have talked to her. Or noticed she wouldn't talk to anyone, if it was like that. They always notice new babies, and compare them, if they have their own there. See if you can get him to show you the book and let you take the names and addresses that come next to hers.'

'I'll get a peek at the book and memorise the names and addresses,' said Reg. 'That's a brilliant idea of yours, Sister.'

He jumped to his feet, eager to get on.

'You won't be able to do it on a Sunday,' said Sister, smiling at his enthusiasm. 'Here, I'll give you the official card with all the days and times he attends at his office. They don't have many births to register there now. He goes round the hospital maternity departments these days to do the registering in the wards. Most mothers go into hospital.'

'I did,' said Mavis.

So Reg had to pace the room and wait while Mavis gave her obstetrical history to the willing and sympathetic ears of Sister. He got her away at last with promises to keep in touch over any further developments in the case of poor Miss Trubb.

A fortnight passed before Reg was able to go to Conington again, this time on a week-day. It meant getting special leave, but he was able to arrange it by taking two days of his annual holiday out of four still owing to him.

'So you see it's paid off, coming back early from Torquay in June,' he told Mavis. 'If I hadn't done that to help them out over that special job, we wouldn't be here now.'

This was at Mrs Ogden's guest house, where they had arrived in time for lunch on Friday, and where they proposed to stay for two nights. The Registrar would be in his office that afternoon. They would see him then.

Mr Coke had given Reg the particulars on the birth certificate of the murdered child. Thomas Trubb, born on August 11th, 1940, the son of Helen Trubb.

'Do you think he'll let us see the book?' Mavis asked. 'It's a long time ago. They may not have it. He'll tell you to go and look in Somerset House.'

'We'll see,' Reg answered. He felt rather doubtful himself, but trusted to his quick wits to use any situation to his own advantage.

The Registrar was puzzled by the unusual request, but, as Reg saw at once, the name of Trubb meant nothing at all to him.

'She's a sort of distant connection,' Reg told him. 'But we lost touch when she had this trouble. I thought if I knew the address and that, we might trace her.'

'After all this time? In any case, why this office? Why not Somerset House? Why not the police? Or even an advertisement in a newspaper?'

'Well, we never exactly knew it was a child. It was just a rumour in the family. My parents never took it up. Too respectable by half. But my wife and I thought. . . . So we went to the District Nurses here, and she certainly did have a kid. So it really was Sister's idea. . . . She said you. . . .'

Reg petered out, invention failing, and sat looking at the Registrar with innocent eyes, and an ingratiating smile on his handsome face. If Mavis had heard all the lies he had just spoken, he thought, he'd never hear the last of it.

The Registrar was fairly new to the job, and not too old

himself to appreciate generosity in those younger than himself.

'You'll have to wait,' he said. 'I must attend to the people outside. Then if there's time I'll see if I can find the entry for you.'

He took down date and name and Reg went back to Mavis in the waiting-room. The presence of several bereaved groups, and two young men who might be fathers, made it impossible for him to tell her exactly what had happened.

'We've got to wait,' was all he said, and relapsed into silence. Mavis asked no questions. She had no wish to bring up Miss Trubb's name before strangers.

An hour later the room was empty, except for the Holmes pair. They sat on, wondering if the Registrar had forgotten them. But after another fifteen minutes he appeared at the door of his office and beckoned them in.

'I said she was a sort of connection,' Reg whispered hurriedly, as they moved forward.

'Of ours? You *didn't!*'

'Sh! He's never heard of her.'

Before Mavis had fully recovered from her indignation they were inside the room and Reg was bending over a large open book on the table.

'That'll be it,' he said. He pulled out an envelope from his pocket and wrote quickly on it. 'Thanks ever so.'

'I hope you'll find the place,' the Registrar said. 'But that part of Conington is very much changed. A great deal of it was heavily bombed in the war. So they tell me. I only came here five years ago, myself.'

'We're very much obliged,' Reg said warmly. 'If this doesn't work we'll have to think of something else.'

The Registrar watched them go. He was beginning to wonder what help he had really given them. The address? But there were other ways of finding it than by looking at a past entry in the Registry of Births. Perhaps he ought to have refused. But the young man had been very plausible. Too plausible. Was the inquiry a fake, and he was just having a look at the office with a view to burglary?

The Registrar, after feeling hot and cold by turns, put down this idea. There was nothing to burgle except the registers, and the petty cash. Nothing worth the trouble, anyway. The safe was a good one.

'Did you get what you wanted?' Mavis asked, as she and Reg walked back towards the bus stop. They had left the car at the guest house to avoid driving in unfamiliar traffic.

'Near enough. I got three names and addresses of people who registered that day. We'll try them tomorrow. Of course they may not have been there at the same time as Miss Trubb. It wasn't only for births, and the deaths would be in a different book.'

So the next morning they set out after breakfast, with Mrs Ogden's directions fresh in their minds, and a little sketch map Reg had made.

Their first call was a failure. No one of the name they asked for lived at that address. The second was also no good. They found the house, a total wreck, in an area still waiting for demolition, with well-grown bushes growing inside its crumbling walls. But their third attempt was more promising.

The house, they discovered, was one of a row in a rather dreary part of the town. Two boys on roller skates were sliding from the door to the edge of the pavement and back, the object apparently being to make a quick turn without falling into the gutter. There were several failures as the Holmeses approached.

'Does Mrs Wetherburn live here?' Reg asked one of the boys, side-stepping to avoid being run down.

'That's right.' The boy skated on to the doorstep, clattered over it, pushing the door open, and shouted, 'Mum! Someone to speak to you!'

A stout middle-aged woman appeared in the doorway, wiping her hands on her apron. She looked at Reg and Mavis with surprise filling her large blue eyes.

'I thought it was the rent,' she said.

Mavis moved forward.

'I hope you'll excuse us, Mrs Wetherburn,' she began. 'I wonder if we could speak to you for a minute.'

'I don't want to buy anything, if that's what you mean,' the stout woman said, with cheerful vigour.

'Oh no, it's not that at all. It's – it's personal,' Mavis said.

This was proving more difficult than she had expected. Mrs Wetherburn's face was already hardening.

'Personal to me, d'you mean?' she asked. 'What's he been up to now?'

Worse and worse. Mavis looked back imploringly at Reg. He stepped forward.

'Personal to us,' he said. 'I can't very well explain out here in the street. If we could just step inside for a minute. It won't take long.'

'Well, I don't know, I'm sure,' said Mrs Wetherburn, now wholly mystified, indignant, but curious. 'You can come into the passage, I suppose. I've got the lounge all upside down. . . . .'

They moved into the narrow passage, including the two boys, who had listened to the conversation with mounting interest.

'Be off, you two!' exclaimed Mrs Wetherburn, seeing their bright faces behind her visitors. 'Nosey young devils!'

She pushed them into the street and shut the door on them.

'Now let's have it,' she said, less amiably than before.

Reg began with a story rather different from the one he had told the Registrar. This time Miss Trubb was a friend of theirs, an old friend with a past that troubled her.

'I'll say it does,' said Mrs Wetherburn, grimly. 'Friend of yours, is she? I don't envy you.'

'You remember her, then?' Mavis asked.

'I remember the case. I had good reason to. They nearly got me into the witness box.'

'Why?'

'Because I'd sat next to her at the Registrar's. I was putting in my first, because my hubby was on night work at the time, and she was there, right beside me, with that poor lamb, just a few weeks old, in her arms. Making out she was that fond of it. And only three years later – '

'She went in to register the baby just before you, did she?'

'How did you know that?'

'Because your name is next to hers in the register.'

'I suppose so.'

'She went in just before you?'

'Oh, *she* didn't go in. Got her sister to do that for her. A

68

lot of whispering went on, and she got out of it by making her sister go in. Ashamed, I suppose, as she had good reason to be.'

'Her sister!' Mavis could not help exclaiming. She turned to Reg with wide eyes. 'But that means – '

He checked her. Mrs Wetherburn was looking at them with a very hostile expression.

'Tell me,' Reg said, in a soothing voice. 'Was this other girl, the sister, you call her, in uniform? Was she in the Forces?'

'Oh, no. Not a bit of it. She *was* her sister, too. There was quite a family likeness between them, and the baby as well. I remarked on it and this Trubb woman said they were sisters.'

'You are very bitter against her,' said Mavis, sadly.

'I don't like hypocrites,' said Mrs Wetherburn, fiercely. 'Sitting there waiting, she gave the impression she was devoted to that child. She told me with tears in her eyes that it had no father. There was no call for her to say anything. We were complete strangers. She went out of her way to say it. And all the time harbouring murderous thoughts. Must have been.'

Reg and Mavis moved away, but at the door he turned round.

'Did you say you nearly had to give evidence?' he asked. 'Was that evidence of your conversation with Miss Trubb?'

'That's right. But they changed their minds. They had plenty of evidence without me, thank goodness. I don't know why they didn't hang her and have done.'

Reg wrote to Mr Warrington-Reeve on Sunday, after he and Mavis got back to Sandfields Avenue. On Monday evening the barrister rang him up.

'About the episode at the registrar's office,' he began. 'We hoped to make something of it, of course. Registrars usually insist on the particulars being given by a parent of the child in question. Frances – Mrs Meadows – told us quite openly that she went in for her sister, in order to spare her the pain and shame of doing it herself. For the same reason she kept the birth certificate for some time in her own possession and did all the necessary business about a ration book, an identity card and so on. Miss Trubb agreed that this was so. Mrs Meadows did not hand the birth certificate over until the time came, a year later, to renew the cards. In case Miss Trubb needed it.'

'She didn't actually show her sister the birth certificate at the time of registration?'

'Apparently not.'

Reg was excited.

'So if the baby was not Miss Trubb's, but was registered as being hers, she wouldn't know that for a year?'

'What are you suggesting?'

'It sticks out a mile! Miss Trubb isn't the sort of woman to let someone else keep something she ought to look after herself. Besides, she'd want to see the thing, if it was her own child. But suppose it wasn't? Suppose it was Frances's baby? Frances saw the registrar because she was the mother, Miss Trubb held the child for her. But Frances gave the name of Helen. Palming the baby off on her sister, don't you see? Or trying to.'

'But it was Helen who called herself Trubb, instead of her real name, Clements.'

'Are you sure of that?'

'Oh yes, she took the name of Trubb as soon as she left her home in Weyford.'

'What about Frances? What did she call herself in those vague jobs before she joined the Forces? What was she in the Forces?'

'Clements, until she married, which was quite soon. I really don't know, before that. I doubt if I went into it.'

Reg groaned.

'No. You wouldn't have to. You were dealing with Helen, not Frances.'

'Exactly. In fact, as I have told you, Frances was quite frank about her activities, including seeing the registrar on Helen's behalf. In any case that was not important, or did not seem so at the time.'

'Not important? That the child could well have belonged to Frances?'

Warrington-Reeve's voice grew icy.

'May I remind you that Miss Trubb was not being tried

for having a baby, but for having killed a child of three who
was in her care. Her sole care. And that she was alone in the
house on the night he died.'

CHAPTER 8

'It's all very well for him to say that,' Reg protested, returning to Mavis and throwing himself into a chair, with all the violence of acute frustration.

'Say what?'

He told her, and waited for her support. She nodded. But his mother-in-law, Mrs Ford, said quietly, 'She was the one with the motive, though. Miss Trubb, I mean. She had the child on her hands. Whether he was hers or not, she had all that responsibility and expense. It would be natural for her to resent it, more particularly if he wasn't her own, and her sister had foisted him off on her by a trick.'

They looked at her with respect and attention. Mrs Ford was one of those very ordinary women who make no brilliant discoveries, who never shine by their own light, but who, patiently and rather slowly, acquire over the years a solid store of knowledge and experience, from which they can draw out conclusions and advice very much to the point on almost any human problem.

Seeing that the young people expected further explanation, Mrs Ford laid her knitting down on her lap and went on.

'You see, a lot of people are capable of a generous action on the spur of the moment. Suppose this Miss Trubb was not the mother. Suppose it really was her sister. But she agreed, out of the goodness of her heart, to look after the child. Not thinking at the time that he would be considered hers. You've said over and over how much she likes little children. Perhaps she took him to avoid going on with war work. Perhaps she thought he'd be better cared for by her than by the other. If that was so, and Frances agreed to let him go, she was right, wasn't she? I mean Miss Trubb. But then time went on. She may never have expected her sister to leave him with her for good. It may have been a temporary arrangement, till the girl got more settled.'

'You are definitely assuming it was Frances's child, aren't you?' asked Reg.

'You told me he could be.'

'Yes, I did. Go on.'

'Well, then, she married, didn't she? This Frances. She married the man Miss Trubb had been friendly with. That must have been a blow to her. But I'd like to know why she didn't make her sister take the child then, or at any rate make her tell her husband. I'd like to know why she didn't confide in this Mr Meadows earlier, when she first knew her sister was in trouble, if she and he were really something to one another. I'd like to know why he never came out on her behalf at the trial.'

'We don't know anything about Colin Meadows, do we?' said Mavis.

'Except he was in old Mr Clements's office,' Reg answered. 'And he and Helen were supposed to be going steady. And he went and married Frances about nine months after the birth of the child.'

'He could have been the father,' said Mrs Ford, 'whichever of them had it. That would account for him keeping out of the whole business.'

'If he behaved like that, he must be a pretty good stinker!'

'Well, I don't know,' Mrs Ford said, mildly. 'There's a lot of men, and girls too, who think it's all the other's fault if anything happens. They forget they share the blame. If it was Miss Trubb, Helen, I think you said her name is, then he may have been disgusted with her for letting him down, as he'd call it, and go off and marry her sister. If it was Frances, he might have married to make it up to her, but not to the extent of taking the baby into his home, and exposing them both. Especially in his position, under her father, and that.'

'I think he ought to have taken the baby, if it was his wife's,' said Mavis, indignantly.

'He must have put her up to palming it off on Helen,' added Reg.

'On account of old Mr Clements,' Mrs Ford insisted.

'Colin had gone into the Forces by that time.'

'All the same, he'd have hoped to come through the war. They all did, except those fighter pilots. And then he'd want his position back, and that would never happen if Mr Clements had got to know what they'd been up to, behind his back, and taking advantage of the opportunities.'

'Still less if it was Helen he'd got the child with,' said Reg.

'Exactly,' agreed Mrs Ford.

They fell silent, considering all they knew. It was not enough. It has hardly anything. All conjecture, really. But it could put Frances in a very queer light. If the child was hers, then she had quite deliberately made it out to be Helen's. She must have given Helen's name, instead of her own, for ration cards, at the Registrar's office, for the baby's identity card. Where else?

'Her identity card!' exclaimed Reg, suddenly. 'If Frances was putting herself across as Helen, unknown to her sister, how did she manage without Helen's identity card?'

'She couldn't,' said Mrs Ford. 'But if you lost your card it wasn't all that difficult to get another.'

'You mean she could pretend she'd lost it. Or take Helen's and get *her* to think she'd lost it?'

'That would be the thing.'

'We *are* making Frances out a terrible character,' cried Mavis, half laughing. 'She didn't seem like that. She was nice and gentle, and very upset over Helen. It sounded genuine to me.'

'She's had a long time to play the part,' said Mrs Ford, quietly. 'You'd expect her to be word perfect by now.'

Seeing the real horror on the young faces before her, she added, 'I'm not saying she did all that. Only that she could. And if she did, it's easy to see that Miss Trubb would grow more and more resentful as time passed, and perhaps think she could never prove her innocence, until in the end she may have got to hate the child, and longed to be free, and decided to do away with him.'

'I don't believe she would, and I never will,' said Mavis.

'Hear, hear,' said Reg.

Mrs Ford smiled at them both and took up her knitting.

A letter to the address in the Lake District brought a polite answer, but no further information. Nurse Walters's parents had lost touch with their daughter. She had chosen to marry in Canada without their knowledge or consent, and when they expressed their disapproval she stopped writing and they had heard nothing since. They could not now recall the address her last letter came from. They had destroyed it without making a note of that.

Reg's next move was to see Miss Trubb's recent employer. The latter had made inquiries at the hospital when he read the paragraph in the newspaper, and being refused a visit to Miss Trubb herself, had decided in the end to write to the address where she had been living. Reg opened this letter, which was addressed 'The Occupier'. He answered it at once, and went to see Mr Philpot one evening after he had finished work.

'I'm very pleased to meet you,' said Mr Philpot, shaking Reg warmly by the hand. 'The Sister at the hospital told me you practically saved Miss Trubb's life, and had behaved very well over the whole thing since.'

'We liked her,' Reg said. He was getting tired of saying this, but it had to be repeated as often as necessary.

'So did I.'

Mr Philpot was an elderly man, but gave an impression of vitality greater than his years normally allowed.

'So did I,' he repeated. 'Very much indeed. Of course I knew all about her.'

'You did?'

'I had to. References, experience, last job and so on. She didn't try to hide anything. But she impressed me very favourably, and I'd just lost a very valuable secretary, through illness. They aren't easy to come by, these days, not the real old-fashioned type, who know all the answers.'

'Wasn't she a bit out of practice?' Reg asked, out of curiosity.

'No. She'd been acting in a secretarial capacity at the prison. Running the library and other jobs. Some of our modern methods were new to her, and the latest machines, but she soon picked them up. I may tell you I was very shocked to know what had happened to her.'

A thought struck Reg with some force.

'She didn't give notice, then? You had no warning?'

'Of course not.'

'She didn't send you a message, as she did us and her sister?'

'No.'

'That wasn't like her. *Unless she didn't mean to leave you.*'

'What d'you mean?'

Reg told him. He found himself explaining the whole affair to Mr Philpot, who did not stop him, but listened with the greatest interest and attention.

'I may be able to help you in one direction,' he said. 'Miss Trubb told me about her war work in Conington. As a matter of fact I know one of the present directors of the same works. They have reverted to civil engineering and I come in contact with them in my export business. I could do a little snooping for you next time I'm up there. Perhaps get dates of when she joined them, when she left, and so on. It seems to me, from what she told me, if I remember it rightly, that she couldn't have carried on as long as she did if she was really pregnant at the time.'

Reg thanked him profusely, and left, feeling he had gained one more, and perhaps this time a very valuable, ally.

His elation was dashed, however, when he reached home that evening. He was met by anxious faces. Mavis and Mrs Ford had had a nasty shock during the afternoon.

'It was like this,' explained the latter. 'I was sitting with my feet up, reading the paper. Mavis had run down to the shops for a loaf, because we'd forgotten earlier on we used the old one in an apple charlotte. Joy was in her pram just outside the window, where I could keep an eye on her. She was sitting up, playing with that rattle she has tied on to the hood. I don't know if I dozed off. I may have, because I heard no steps on the path or anything. But I was surprised all of a sudden to hear Joy chuckling. You know – the way she does if anyone tickles her or when you throw her about,

Reg. I turned my head and there was someone standing in the garden, waving her hands about and grinning. It gave me an awful turn. I couldn't move for a minute, my legs felt like jelly. When I did manage to get up and go to the window, there was no one there, and Joy was still sitting in her pram throwing her rattle around.'

'Sure you didn't dream it?' asked Reg, with a sceptical smile.

'No,' said Mavis. 'She didn't. I met Rita Williams in the street when I'd just come out of Smithers with my loaf and she said, "I had a surprise this morning. Who do you think I saw going into Dr Evenett's? Your Miss Trubb. I didn't know she was back." I said, "She isn't with us," and she said, "I didn't think she would be. I wouldn't have thought she'd show her face in these parts again." So I said, "Nor would I. Anyway we haven't seen her." When I got back and Mum said a strange woman had been inside the garden close to Joy's pram, I nearly dropped.'

'Are you sure it was Miss Trubb?' Reg asked, though he felt pretty certain now that it must have been their late lodger.

'I've never seen her, of course,' said Mrs Ford, 'but your description fitted her to a tee. Clothes and all.'

'You only caught a glimpse of her?'

'That's right. But it flashed through my mind at once, "That must be Miss Trubb." Otherwise I wouldn't have felt so frightened.'

'Yes,' said Reg gloomily.

'Anyway, Rita wouldn't be mistaken,' Mavis added, 'so she was definitely in the district. I think we ought to tell the police she was here, trespassing.'

'She didn't do any harm,' said Reg, unwillingly. 'Why are we all against her, now? You know we've always said she would never harm Joy.'

'I don't know what to think,' said Mavis, and her eyes filled with distracted tears.

After he had comforted her, Reg gave the two women an account of his conversation with Mr Philpot, and in their concentration on what they were hearing, they forgot their recent fright and the importance they had given to Miss Trubb's brief reappearance.

'So,' concluded Reg, 'I hope we'll hear something about her when she was first in Conington, before the baby was born. The next thing I'd like to know is what Frances was like at that time, or earlier. We've heard that Colin was Helen's boy friend. What about the sister? At an art school, didn't we hear? Seems to me if Frances was in with a lot of art students she must have found a boy friend or two among them.'

'Of an undesirable type, I should think,' said Mrs Ford, who held the conventional British view that art of any kind was both peculiar and disreputable.

'Not in Weyford,' said Mavis. 'Not at a little art school like that one, only for the locals. Not like in London – or Paris,' she added, with a little knowing laugh.

They all laughed. But Reg agreed entirely with what she said.

'It won't be easy to find out anything there,' he said, 'unless Mrs Meadows helps us. And I hardly like to ask her, when the object is to see if she could have had a baby with one of her early pals.'

Mrs Ford was shocked.

'I don't see that you've any excuse for prying into Mrs Meadows's past,' she said. 'If there was anything, she'd have the law on you for defamation of character.'

'Not if it was true, she couldn't,' said Mavis.

A thought struck Reg. A new and exciting possibility.

'Blackmail!' he said. 'Now there's a motive!'

'What d'you mean?'

'Suppose Frances had the child and palmed it off on Miss Trubb who couldn't bring herself to name her as the mother after she heard Frances had married her old sweetheart. Suppose the father of the child started blackmailing Frances, so she killed it, to remove the grounds for blackmail.'

'Bringing the whole thing into the open, with maximum publicity,' declared Mavis.

'It was meant to look like an accident, wasn't it? Only they don't smother themselves at three years of age.'

'Far-fetched,' went on Mavis. 'You don't even know if it *was* hers. And if it was, it didn't have to be blackmail from outside. It could just be fear that Miss Trubb might give her away.'

'I think the whole idea is screwy,' said Mrs Ford. 'I can see a kind-hearted woman looking after her sister's child. I can't see her risking her own life to save a murderess, sister or no sister. I should say no one would do that, unless they were a bit mental.'

'I suppose not,' said Reg, sadly, and added, 'anyway, as the barrister chap said, it doesn't matter whose child it was, Miss Trubb was alone with it at the time it was killed.'

He looked so depressed that Mavis felt she must encourage his new idea, however far-fetched it was.

'Never mind,' she said. 'You try it out. This blackmail idea. Can't Mr Warrington-Reeve tell you anything about Frances's early life? He must have followed up the idea of her having a boy friend. Why don't you ask him?'

'I'll do that,' said Reg, feeling more cheerful.

Mr Warrington-Reeve was interested to hear the result of Reg's second visit to Conington and his contact with Mr Philpot. He was frankly puzzled by Miss Trubb's brief reappearance. He was able to confirm that Frances had indeed made many friends at the Weyford art school; in fact she was quite notorious there for the short time, only a year, during which she attended its classes. At the time of the trial he had got in contact with several of these young men. One had gone on to London, being unfit for military service, and was believed to be still working there, though his efforts were spasmodic and he had made no great name for himself. The others had disappeared in the war, or after it had changed their ideas and ambitions and attempted other careers, or thankfully subsided into safe jobs. Several of these still lived in their home town.

'It was a fairly amateurish kind of art school,' Warrington-Reeve explained. 'Run by a talented crank who couldn't work in with other people. He managed to wangle some sort of grant out of the Town Council, which had a leaning towards culture with a capital C. The Council changed its mind, naturally, in the war, and the art school faded away.'

'You seem to know a lot about it,' said Reg. 'You must have been taking steps already.'

The barrister laughed.

'You inspired the effort,' he said. 'And our excellent Mr Coke supplied the details as far as he could extract them his end.'

Reg considered.

'Wasn't that a bit risky? I mean, if there's someone who doesn't want us to know about him, he may have been warned.'

'Just so. But as I said before, up to a point we want to encourage self-revelation.'

'Up to a point, I agree. But it's a danger point, isn't it? For me and my family?'

Warrington-Reeve's dark eyes flashed.

'You can always retire from the fray, can't you? If you don't like it.'

'That means you're going on?'

The other nodded.

'With the utmost discretion,' he said. 'And it may interest you to know that the unsuccessful artist, the early friend, or I ought to say, one of the early friends of Frances Clements, lives not very far from you in the Wimbledon area. I'll give you his address. It is possible that he met Miss Trubb by chance as she was on her way to work, and recognized her. It is possible that he made himself known to her.'

'Blackmail!' cried Reg. 'A reason for her attempted suicide. No,' he checked himself. 'It wasn't suicide. Too much against it. All wrong, the way it was done.'

'Unless she is unbalanced,' said Warrington-Reeve.

'She's not mental,' answered Reg. 'She's as sane as you or me.'

'In that connection,' said the barrister, 'I think you had better just let Inspector Brown know of her unexpected and rather peculiar visit to your garden.'

Reg did this the same day. Inspector Brown looked at him, kindly.

'That's right,' he said. 'More than likely it was the lady in question. She certainly went to Dr Evenett's surgery that morning, as your wife's friend alleges. She was admitted to a mental hospital that evening, as a voluntary patient. So you can set your mind at rest for the present, can't you?'

CHAPTER 9

Mrs Ford welcomed the news of Miss Trubb's admission to hospital with feelings of considerable relief.

'You won't be wanting me any longer,' she told her daughter as they were making the beds together the next morning.

'We always like having you here,' Mavis assured her, truthfully.

'I know, dear. I'm a lucky old woman, and you are a lucky young one, having a man like Reg to look after you.'

Mavis was moved to walk round the end of the bed and kiss her mother for the double compliment. After which Mrs Ford repeated, calmly, 'With her being properly looked after, there's no more danger for Joy.'

'I don't know about that,' Mavis protested. 'We think it might be someone else.'

'It was her in the garden,' argued Mrs Ford. 'Anyway, I'd like to get back and see how the place has been getting on without me.'

'It'll be all right,' said Mavis. 'It's barely a fortnight.'

'Long enough for the dust to collect.'

'Well, we'll see what Reg has to say.'

Reg did not say much. He liked Mrs Ford staying with them, because it was lonely through the day for Mavis. But he also liked having his wife to himself, as his mother-in-law was very well aware. She agreed to stay over the week-end, and then left on Monday morning. Reg drove her to Wimbledon Station and saw her off before going on to work.

Mavis found the house very empty and quiet that morning,

but it was Monday, with the laundry to organize, and soon the washing machine was humming away and she forgot the loneliness in planning food for the next twenty-four hours.

Carol Fry rang her up at lunch-time, inviting her to bring Joy over to tea. Inevitably they discussed Miss Trubb.

'Would you really take Joy, if she'll let me go and see her?'

'Of course I will. Dump her here any time.'

'I'll see if I can have the car. Reg doesn't always take it to work. In fact, hardly ever. We're very well served with buses.'

'You do that, then.'

So Mavis wrote to the hospital, asking if she would be allowed to see Miss Trubb, as an old friend, though not a relation, and if so, when it would be convenient. An answer came after a few days, to say that Miss Trubb was making satisfactory progress, and that she was willing to see Mrs Holmes at the usual visiting hour. Mavis made her arrangements accordingly.

Miss Trubb walked slowly in the grounds of Flowerfield Hospital, absorbed in her own thoughts. She was feeling calmer than on the day when a sudden panic had driven her to Dr Evenett's surgery, but she was still profoundly troubled.

Two fears held her swaying between two abysses of terror, and the deeper one was not on her own account, or was only indirectly so. If anything happened to Joy, she would be blamed. The old nightmare, driven down and nearly forgotten for so many years, had risen in a new guise, and sent her flying before its cruel impact on her mind and heart.

She hoped she had made good provision to guard against both sources of danger. She remembered, with a grim half-smile playing round her thin lips, how Dr Evenett had stared at her when she told him her life was in danger. He was aware that it had been in danger, he told her, very slowly and gently, as one would speak to a child. But wasn't that by her own act? She remembered his total disbelief when she refused the responsibility; when she told him that the gas had been a deliberate attempt on her life, regardless of the others in the house, who providentially, had not been there. Who, he asked, could have wanted to take her life? And she had to answer, untruthfully, that she had no idea, and to watch

83

his disbelief in the facts change into a firm conviction of her delusion.

So it had been easy, after a few more seemingly preposterous statements, to break down, to cry a little, to stammer out that she was afraid her brain was giving way, finally to beg him to send her to a mental hospital for treatment. Dr Evenett had agreed, rather too quickly, she thought. So here she was, at the end of a week's observation in bed, promoted to life in a villa, with a number of other mild anxiety cases to keep her company, and with a measure of comfortable freedom. So far so good.

Miss Trubb's intense recollection, living again every minute of a chosen episode, was a habit or accomplishment she had perfected during her first year in prison. It had seemed to her then, a young woman of twenty-four, that her life was over. It had seemed necessary to fix in her mind all the sights and sounds of her past, as if she were suddenly become deaf and blind; to recall and fasten in her memory all the living emotions, the joys, even the sorrows, of the existence now shut away beyond the prison walls, so that she might continually play over these scenes, like gramophone records; or watch them, like pictures on the screen, or better still, like plays at the theatre, with living actors before her. For in all of them she took the chief part, and she wanted her performance to be a true one, a replica of the actual one she had given, at home, at school, with her mother and father, with Colin. And with Frances.

That name, coming as it always did, at the end of the cycle of her thoughts, snapped down the curtain and ended the play. Nothing followed, no thoughts, no scenes, no action. Only a great wave of misery, from which she was accustomed to struggle out most painfully, half drowned in her despair.

Before she was released Miss Trubb had grown used to these changes in herself, so that she hardly noticed them, and being a good deal alone, not interrupted, suffered no discomfort from her withdrawal. Afterwards she had responded more easily than she feared to the demands of her new life. She had been especially grateful to the Holmeses for leaving her alone as much as they did. The could not have treated her more gently if they had known the whole truth of her life, she thought. It was not until the night of their party, and the dreadful visit –

She refused to tell the psychiatrist who this visitor was. Her plan for the future was not yet complete. She was still running away. If, later, if she was driven at last to turn and fight, then it would be a matter for the police. But not yet. Not yet.

'Miss Trubb has agreed to see you,' said the psychiatrist who was treating her. 'I'm afraid we have not made much of her case, yet. She has a vague persecution mania, and some fairly obvious delusions. But she is at an unstable age, of course.'

'Anyone would be liable to get unstable after what she's been through,' said Mavis, defensively.

'Oh, quite, quite.' The psychiatrist hastened to explain that he was not unsympathetic, adding, 'I can see that you know her fairly well, and are not likely to upset her. I have heard the outline of her history from Inspector Brown. Perhaps you can add to it.'

'No. She never told us a thing about herself. Not a thing.'

'I see. The Inspector told me that you and your husband had started up some sort of investigation into her past. He thought it was a mistake.'

'I bet,' said Mavis. 'They wouldn't like to be shown up to be wrong from the start. Her barrister doesn't think it's a mistake. He's quite keen. And her boss. And her landlady at the time of the – when the child died. Everyone, really, except the woman at the Registrar's office, who thought she'd been deceitful and cowardly, letting her sister go in to do the registering.'

'Her sister,' said the doctor, thoughtfully. Miss Trubb had refused to see Mrs Meadows, and it had been quite difficult to prevent the latter from making her own way into the ward, even in the face of this refusal. But it was not a topic to discuss with young Mrs Holmes.

'So you think we ought to stop?' Mavis asked.

This sounded rather abrupt, so she went on, 'Me and my husband don't think she's bats at all.'

'I see,' said the doctor, shortly.

He pushed a bell on his desk and a nurse appeared.

'Take Mrs Holmes to see Miss Trubb,' he said, getting up and holding out a limp hand to Mavis. She took it, hoping she would never go round the bend herself, if this cold fish of a man was the sort of doctor that treated you. So different from cheery Dr Evenett.

'Will you come this way,' said the nurse, kindly.

Mavis followed. She was pleasantly surprised. No locks, no bars, no clanging doors. But then Miss Trubb wasn't very bad.

'Where do you keep the really bad ones?' she asked the nurse. 'The violent ones?'

The girl, quite young, laughed cheerfully.

'We don't have any,' she said. 'Or hardly ever. There are special wards and isolation wards in the hospital block. They all go to bed for observation to begin with, and for treatment to be started. Miss Trubb didn't need anything much. She's absolutely harmless.'

'That's what we're sure of,' agreed Mavis, fervently. The nurse gave her a curious look, but said nothing.

Miss Trubb showed no surprise when Mavis arrived in the visitors' room. She was sitting down when the nurse brought Mavis in, and she stood up at once, but did not move forward. The girl saw that she was wearing her own clothes, the dark rather rusty blue suit, and grey overcoat. But no hat.

'I've been walking in the grounds,' said Miss Trubb. 'I walk a lot. It does me good.'

'I'll leave you with Mrs Holmes,' said the nurse. 'Doctor told me not more than twenty minutes.'

Mavis sat down and Miss Trubb slowly copied her. There was an awkward silence. Mavis had not realized how difficult it was to begin. There was the gas business, and there was the inquiry. It seemed impossible to say anything about either. But Miss Trubb came to the rescue.

'I'm so sorry,' she said, gently, in the voice that Mavis had grown to like and respect, 'that you had all the inconvenience and publicity of my – illness. It was not my fault, and I could not have prevented it.'

Mavis mumbled something to the effect that it was Miss Trubb, not herself and Reg. who had suffered.

'Thank God,' said Miss Trubb, solemnly. 'I could not have prevented it unless I had left your house at once, after – '

She stopped suddenly, her eyes widening as she saw where her softened feelings were leading her.

'After what?' asked Mavis, gently. 'Do tell me, Miss Trubb. We – we wish you'd let us help, Reg and me. We'd do anything – honestly. We felt so bad about it all, afterwards. We thought we'd let you down, somehow.'

'Oh, no,' cried Miss Trubb, clasping her hands together, her face working. 'Don't say things like that! I mustn't tell you anything – ever!'

Tears had begun to roll down her cheeks. Mavis felt both alarmed and guilty. She began to tell Miss Trubb about Joy's latest progress; how well and firmly she sat up on the floor; how she could roll over on her back if you put her down on her tummy, and nearly roll over on her tummy when she was lying on her back. Miss Trubb encouraged this sort of talk, and soon heard all about Mrs Ford's visit and what Reg had been doing in the garden. Mavis wanted to ask if Miss Trubb had managed to get away from the hospital to visit them, and if so why she had not come in, but she was afraid to bring on another fit of crying. Besides, Miss Trubb began to tell her about her own comfortable life in the hospital.

'We have parole,' explained Miss Trubb, calmly, 'which makes a nice change from always going round the grounds.'

'What's parole?'

'You give your word you'll come back in by a certain time. Otherwise they don't mind where you go. To the shops, or – well – anywhere.'

Mavis sat and stared. Why didn't she mention her visit to the garden just before she went into hospital? Why didn't she offer to come and see them, now? For a horrid moment, the security, the confidence, even the faith in Miss Trubb, withered and shrank. It must have been her in the garden. It could have been her before that – the note on the pram. And any time now – with Mum not there to help.

'Then it *was* you!' she heard herself saying, at the moment the nurse opened the door and came in, smiling.

Mavis sprang up. The nurse did not seem to have heard. She merely said, 'Time, I'm afraid.' Mavis turned back, ashamed of her doubts, holding out her hand.

But Miss Trubb was sitting huddled down on her chair, her head bent, her eyes on the floor.

'Miss Trubb, I — I didn't mean — ' Mavis began. But the nurse plucked at her sleeve, guiding her to the door.

'Don't take any notice,' she whispered. 'They're all liable to act like this. I expect she's tired. You're her first visitor since she came here.'

Mavis went home, thoroughly discouraged by this interview, and for the first time persuaded that their late lodger was far from normal.

'Don't you think it might be the surroundings?' Reg asked, hiw own faith still unshaken. 'You must have seen some of the real loonies.'

'You can't tell, really. Quite a lot of people were in the grounds as I went in, but they looked the same as anyone else. Well, yes, I did see a few who looked different. Too blank, if you see what I mean, or too eager. I don't want to think about them. The point is, she goes in and out just as she likes. And it's only a sixpenny bus ride from here.'

'What of it?'

'Do you think it's safe? I felt awful this morning. I kept running out into the garden, even though I could see the pram from the windows.'

'I think it's safe.'

'We never found out who put the note on the pram, though, did we? And we haven't stopped making inquiries.'

'I don't see how anyone could know we hadn't stopped. Mr Coke and Mr Warrington-Reeve and Inspector Brown are the only ones who know what we've been doing. We haven't been to Weyford again.'

'We have been to Conington. That's the awful part of it!' Mavis cried, in desperation. 'Not knowing where the link is. Or even if it's through Frances or through Helen. It would be much simpler if we decided it was all Helen.'

'Someone decided the same thing sixteen years ago,' said Reg, grimly. 'And I want to find the bastard that did.'

Two days later Mavis took Joy in her pram in the afternoon to a small public garden not very far from Sandfields Avenue, but in the older part of the district. There she met Rita Williams, who was playing with her own small son, aged two. A big rug was spread on the grass, and the two children sat down on it, while their mothers found a public bench close by.

Presently young Derek got up and wandered off. Rita, who was expecting her second child, sighed wearily.

'I'll bring him back,' said Mavis. She got up and followed Derek at a distance, deciding not to catch him up until he had exhausted his present burst of energy. But a warning call from Rita made her turn round. The latter was coming quickly across the grass.

'He goes for the water,' she called. 'Past those trees.'

Mavis remembered the pond at once. She had not thought of it so far as a hazard, but now she broke into a run. Rita hurried along behind.

They caught the truant on the far side of the trees. Naturally he was furious at being stopped so near the fulfilment of a fixed obsession. It was several minutes before the two girls stopped his cries and struggles and were able to start back towards their former resting place.

As they left the trees Mavis screamed suddenly and began to run. The garden bench was there, the rug was on the grass. But the pram and the baby had disappeared.

Reg, summoned from his works at four o'clock, found his wife incoherent with shock and grief, Rita Williams in a similar state, and Inspector Brown patiently trying to make sense of their painful exclamations.

Mavis grew calmer with Reg's support and encouragement, and between them the two girls managed to describe what had happened.

'We couldn't have left her more than five minutes,' Rita insisted. 'She was only out of sight a few seconds. It was my fault leaving Joy on the rug, but I'm so scared of that pond! Derek's a persistent little devil!'

'Yes, we were in sight practically the whole time,' Mavis sobbed. 'There wasn't a soul anywhere near us.'

'Except that man,' Rita said.

'What man?' The question came sharply from both Reg and the Inspector.

'Oh, you mean the one in the grey overcoat and the squashy felt hat?' Mavis remembered.

'Sure it was a man?' asked Brown. He was upset by this incident. He had passed off the warning as a hoax. If this kidnapping was a hoax, it was a very serious one. 'Grey overcoat, squashy hat. What colour trousers?' he demanded.

The girls exchanged an embarrassed glance.

'He was in some bushes,' Rita explained. 'I didn't see his trousers.'

'You couldn't very well stare,' said Mavis, 'in the circumstances. But it wasn't Miss Trubb, if that's what you mean. I'd recognize her anywhere.'

'All right, Mrs Holmes. Was that the only person you remember seeing?'

'Yes.'

Rita agreed. There was nothing further to add. Inspector Brown promised to ring them as soon as the child was found. In an hour or two, he said. And then, seeing the stony look on Reg's face, added, 'Just as soon as we get any information.'

Rita went home with Derek, still blaming herself for her own conduct. There was nothing the bereaved parents could do. Brown rang them up shortly after he got back to the Station to say that Miss Trubb was out on parole, but they had not picked her up yet. He would ring again when they did so.

At Joy's usual bedtime Mavis flung herself into Reg's arms, sobbing and shaking in uncontrollable distress. It was getting dark. She thought of her child, lost, perhaps abandoned in the open, perhaps ill-treated, or even already dead. She felt as if she herself were being riven apart, disintegrating, dying.

Suddenly Reg loosened his grip, slipped from Mavis's clinging arms and moved quickly to the window. Staring dumbly out into the garden over her bowed head from the still unlighted room, he had seen the side gate open.

'Come here!' he said, tensely. Mavis ran to his side.

The gate was certainly open, and into the gap came a stout figure in a grey overcoat, moving backwards, and drawing after it a child's pram, with the hood up and the mackintosh cover in place.

Reg flung open the window, and bounded through it into the garden.

'Where's Mavis?' asked Miss Trubb, severely.

'What the hell d'you mean – '

'Mavis had no business to leave Joy all by herself in a public place,' continued Miss Trubb. She had turned the pram and was beginning to push it towards the house. 'It might have been dangerous. You were warned, weren't you?'

Reg took a firm hold on himself. Every instinct, every argument told him Miss Trubb was out of her mind. But she was looking at him with those kind sensible eyes of hers, and her voice was as reasonable as it had ever been.

'How do you know that?' he found himself asking.

'Never mind how. Where's Mavis? Why doesn't she come out?'

Reg was furious.

'You know all the answers, don't you? Then why don't you put an end to all this – this nonsense! Why don't you tell the truth, and put an end to it all?'

For a second Miss Trubb's face crumpled.

'If only I could!' she whispered. 'If only I could!'

Then Mavis was there, putting down the hood, tearing back the cover, lifting out the sleeping baby with little animal cries of mingled pain and joy.

'Take her in and put her to bed,' said Miss Trubb, in her usual calm voice. 'I wouldn't bother to bath her tonight.'

They were too astounded to answer her.

'This will mean losing my parole, I expect,' Miss Trubb continued. 'I shall be back late. I expect you have told the police, too. So you must be much more careful in future. Because this means I shall not be able to keep watch over you any longer.'

CHAPTER 10

Inspector Brown was considerably dashed when Reg rang him up to say that Joy was safe at home, and had been wheeled there in her pram, apparently quite openly, by Miss Trubb.

The Inspector went straight to his Superintendent with this disturbing news, and they agreed that their whole local Force had let them down. They had known that Miss Trubb was out on parole; they had her description, and that of the child and her pram. Yet Miss Trubb had been able to walk out of those public gardens and hide herself and the child somewhere for several hours. Or perhaps she had simply walked about the district unnoticed, and then made her way to Sandfields Avenue.

On further consideration they decided that it was, in fact, only too easy for her. The Force was considerably under strength, as usual. Those highly respectable suburban avenues and roads and crescents were not patrolled closely, if at all. There had been a constable half a mile away from Sandfields Avenue, at the junction of the shopping area and one of the main bus routes. Naturally Miss Trubb would be more likely to see him in such a crowded spot than he would be to see her. And even more naturally, it had not occurred to any of them to put a guard on number Twenty-six. Miss Trubb's action was entirely unexpected.

'That's the worst of these loonies,' sighed the Superintendent. 'You can't anticipate their actions as you can with criminals.'

Inspector Brown gave him a very queer look.

'Doesn't Trubb rate as a criminal?' he asked, softly.

The Superintendent reddened.

'You know what I mean,' he snapped.

'Only too well. That's what worries me.'

'How?'

'All along, since the gas episode, she's been perfectly consistent. Someone wants to get rid of her, now she's free, and that someone wants to scare off these young fools, Reg and Mavis Holmes, for trying to get to the bottom of it. That's what she implies. You know they've been to Warrington-Reeve, her counsel at the trial? And to her sister?'

'Yes. Reeve got on to Mitchell at the Yard, to warn him – that was how he put it – that the Trubb case was active again. I think I'll have a word with Mrs Meadows myself.'

'In the meantime I'll have a word with the top notch at Flowerfield. These psychiatrists don't seem able to see things at the receiving end of their patients' actions.'

'Exactly.'

'I'll try to get them to keep her under control until we sort this out. It'd be a help, even if nothing further transpires.'

In the event it was Inspector Brown who went to Weyford. Mrs Meadows appeared to be very shocked by the news he brought her. The kidnapping incident had been over too quickly to attract the attention of the Press. The hospital doctor had not seen fit to get in touch with her.

'He may be going to write,' she said. 'But you'd have thought he might have rung me up. Though I'm not responsible in any way. It isn't as if she was certified. I – I don't find him very sympathetic, I'm afraid.'

'In what way?'

Mrs Meadows's eyes filled with tears. Her gentle voice roughened.

'He won't let me see Helen.'

'In spite of her wishes?'

'That's just it. She doesn't want to see me. She never does. I used to visit her at the prison regularly, and of course she had to see me then, because the wardress brought her in. But she never spoke. I wish – ' Mrs Meadows's lip trembled, but she controlled herself, and went on. 'Even in those days –

well, right from the beginning, I felt sure she was not normal. Since she came out I'm even more sure. But they won't certify her. I can't understand it. It would be so much better for her.'

'Would it?'

To his surprise the Inspector found himself suddenly on Miss Trubb's side in this matter. He remembered her clear account of all she knew about the gas incident, and even in this recent business over little Joy. Sitting in an isolation room at Flowerfield she had told him quite calmly and very sensibly how she had kept the Holmes family under observation all the hours she was away from the hospital. How she had watched Mavis and her friend leave Joy sitting unattended on a rug, while they went right out of sight. And how, realizing all at once that the child was in danger, she had put her into the pram and wheeled it away.

But there were inconsistencies. She could have wheeled Joy *towards* her mother, not right out of the gardens, giving everyone a fright. And before, over the attempted suicide, he remembered thinking how queer it was that anyone so sensible should have gone about the business in such a haphazard manner, turning on the gas cooker in the kitchen instead of the gas fire in her own room. The reasonable, clear thought and speech, and the stupid action. Did they add up to madness, or to what she insisted upon, an attack from outside? At this moment her sister's conviction and solicitude roused in him a violent support for the latter explanation.

And then to Brown's further surprise he saw that his blunt question and implied doubt had stung Mrs Meadows into direct anger. Her handsome face stiffened, and a gleam of malice shone in her eyes as she answered, 'That is very old-fashioned of you, Inspector. They treat them so well these days. It is a hospital, not an asylum in the old sense.'

'But no liberty,' said Brown, obstinately. 'She's entitled to some, don't you think, after fifteen years?'

Mrs Meadows had no answer to this. Her tears flowed instead. She was genuinely distressed and Inspector Brown apologized for his bluntness. She became calmer.

'If only she had been able to live quietly,' she said. 'I understand she found a very good position with a Mr Philpot.

We lost sight of her completely for those months after she was freed. If she is normal, why did she suddenly try to kill herself?'

'That is what everyone would like to know. Particularly her doctors and the young couple she was living with.'

'The Holmeses. Yes, they came here to see me.'

'I know that.'

Again Mrs Meadows showed instant surprise, but as quickly as before her face relaxed.

'Yes, of course. The kidnapping.'

'No, from the start. Didn't they tell you?'

'I don't think so. I don't remember. I tried to help them, though it seemed to me rather officious on their part. Helen is none of their business.'

'Their house was full of gas. They might have been in it.'

'Oh, surely!' Mrs Meadows clasped her hands together. 'Surely Helen would never have been so wicked – or mad – as to murder her kind landlord and his family in her attempt to kill herself!'

The tables had been turned on him very neatly and thoroughly, Brown thought. He called at the Weyford police station to have a word with his opposite number, Inspector Frost, and then left the town in a thoughtful frame of mind.

With the help of Mr Coke, Warrington-Reeve had been able to trace several more Weyford friends of the young Frances Clements. Mr Coke knew where the disgruntled head of the former art school was living, and from him the barrister learned rather more about the two most prominent admirers of his flighty pupil. Frances had been a disturbing element in his school, he wrote. Anything more Mr Reeve wanted to know must be communicated by word of mouth and treated as a strict confidence. Warrington-Reeve, made suitably curious by this cautious approach, paid the suggested visit and was well rewarded.

He found the former art master all agog to describe his students, and full of curiosity about the barrister's purpose. In this he was unsatisfied, for Warrington-Reeve gave nothing away, though the old man's first statement was a distinct surprise. One of Frances's most favoured friends, it appeared, was a youth called Leslie Coke, a cousin of a solicitor in the town. He had no real talent, left at the beginning of the war, was severely wounded in a commando raid, and subsequently took up accountancy, for which he was much better equipped.

'But you will have heard this already,' he said, with malice, 'unless Stephen Coke has kept it from you.'

Warrington-Reeve made no answer, so the art master continued.

The other principal admirer was also a Weyford lad, an extremely talented, but chronically idle, young person. He was conscripted in due course, and invalided out of the Army following a nervous breakdown. Thereafter he had continued his career of painting in the intervals of sponging on his relations. He was beginning to be known, however, for his early works, considered too outrageously *avant-garde* at the time they were executed, were now finding favour, and often sold for quite large sums. Some of them were finding their way into provincial art galleries. Lack of concentration and over-indulgent living had stopped his progress, but he still painted when the fit took him, and was thought of quite highly in some quarters. He lived in South London, avoiding on purpose the usual haunts of painters. He occasionally wrote to his old master, usually in an unsuccessful attempt to borrow money.

This description filled out the one Mr Coke had already given. The address supplied was near Wimbledon.

For some days after this visit the barrister considered how best to use his information. He found it embarrassing to learn that one possible father of Frances's illegitimate child, supposing her to have had one at all, was related to the very solicitor who had briefed him in defence of Helen. Of course nothing was ever said in those early days about Frances's personal affairs, except in relation to Helen. Perhaps Stephen Coke knew nothing about his young cousins's affairs either. And certainly Leslie was not likely to revive any pre-war scandal about Frances, now that she was so respectably married to the successful and prosperous Colin Meadows. There was nothing to be uneasy about. And yet – and yet –

Warrington-Reeve dismissed his unworthy doubts about

Stephen, but it did occur to him that it might be awkward if he wanted to ask the accountant cousin about his former relations with Mrs Meadows. Whether Leslie was a close friend of Stephen or not, they did both live in Weyford still, and were likely to be in touch to some extent. Warrington-Reeve decided to pursue the other scent first. In any case it was more promising.

Raymond Thorne was very much as the art master had described him: a man of parts gone disastrously to seed.

Warrington-Reeve found him in a dilapidated house, let in floors, standing in a decayed garden behind a high wall, on the borders of a new estate about two miles from Sandfields Avenue. Thorne lived at the top of the house in an attic room where the skylight window served him for his painting. He appeared to have reached that stage in chronic alcoholism where it is not possible at any given moment to decide if the subject is drunk or sober. But he remembered Frances Clements.

'Red-haired bitch,' he said, solemnly. 'Distinctly nympho. Bullied at home by her elder sister. Or so she always said. Attractive, or so I thought at the time. We were both very young, of course.'

He sighed, and liking the effect, sighed again, overdoing it, which made him first belch, then laugh loudly.

'I wasn't the only one,' he added, with meaning.

'So I understand.'

Thorne looked suspicious.

'What's this in aid of? I don't think I quite like you getting my address out of that old fool. False pretences. I thought you wanted to buy a picture.'

'I might, at that,' said Warrington-Reeve, coolly.

'Then why don't you look at some, instead of turning up my past?'

'It's all connected in a way. Did you know the sister, Helen Clements?'

'Did I not! Who could help it? She was a *cause célèbre*. You must know that.'

'I defended her.'

Thorne's expression changed. Either he had kept his wits

in spite of the alcohol, or he was not as far gone as he made out to be.

'So that's it. Her attempted suicide. I saw that in the paper, of course. Only I don't quite see where Frances and I come in.'

'Did you see Helen in this neighbourhood?'

Thorne met this frankly.

'Yes, I did. I saw her in the road one day and I followed her to where she was staying. I don't think she saw me, or recognized me, anyway.'

'Why did you follow her?'

'Curiosity.'

'Did you go later, when you knew where she lived, to pay her a visit?'

'Why should I? It was Frances I'd known, and that was too long ago to remember.'

'But you remembered Miss Trubb. Well enough to recognize her after fifteen years. What did you want from her?'

'Want from her? Nothing.'

His voice was rising. Warrington-Reeve pursued relentlessly.

'Did you want her to give you money? You are always asking people for money, aren't you? Was it blackmail you were considering?'

Thorne heaved himself up, choking with fury.

'Get out!' he shouted, moving towards the older man, fists up. 'Get out of here!'

'There is no need to get excited,' said the barrister, not moving.

Thorne dropped back into his chair.

'It's a lie!' he cried. 'If she says I went to the house, it's a bloody lie! I was away at the time. I can prove it!'

'At what time? When were you away?'

'The week she tried to gas herself.' His recovery was too obvious. Warrington-Reeve stared at him, with contempt in his dark eyes.

'At the time of Miss Trubb's trial,' he said, evenly, 'you were in hospital. I know that. You did not come into the case at all. There was nothing to connect you with Miss Trubb, or with the child. But now we are moving towards a different view of the case. We are looking for the father of that child.'

'*Me!*' Thorne began to laugh, loudly, coarsely, his gross body heaving. 'Me and Helen! Have a heart! I hardly knew her at all.'

'You would not need to,' said the barrister coolly, 'since Miss Trubb was probably *not* the child's mother.'

The laughter stopped abruptly. For a second panic looked out of the artist's red-rimmed eyes. Then he pulled himself together.

'She denied it right through,' he said. 'Yes, I remember that. But it didn't do her any good.'

'At that time, no,' said Warrington-Reeve. 'On the other hand the double murder didn't come off. She was reprieved, not hanged. Now, I am afraid her life is again threatened, for the same reason and by the same person or persons, the true parents of that child. The truth is always hard to find, but we mean to dig it up this time, Coke and I.'

The big man's mouth quivered and fell open.

'Coke?' he said, hoarsely.

'The solicitor who briefed me. Stephen Coke.'

He turned to go. Thorne watched him from his chair, not moving.

'I don't advise it,' he said. 'You're sticking your neck out, you and that young fool couple. Helen's done the sensible thing. Gone to earth. You leave her alone. Better for everyone.'

Warrington-Reeve did not answer. He went down the stairs and out of the house and back to his chambers. He had several new ideas to consider.

Towards the end of the same week, the Holmeses had an unexpected visitor in the shape of Colin Meadows. He rang up Mavis one morning, saying that he was in London for the day on business, and would be glad if he might call in the evening to see her and her husband.

This was the first time either of them had met Mr Meadows. He agreed fairly well with their expectations; a soberly-dressed, middle-aged man, with a rather wooden face, thinning fair hair very carefully brushed, and a quiet manner.

Reg let him in and brought him into the sitting-room. He lost no time in coming to the point.

'I felt I had to see you both,' he said, quietly accepting a cigarette and finding his lighter, 'because my wife is getting extremely nervy and upset as a result of your very well-meant activities, and I think they ought to stop. Especially now that the police have the inquiry in hand.'

The cool authoritative note in his voice immediately kindled a flame of obstinate dissent in Reg.

'I'm sorry Mrs Meadows is upset,' he said. 'You can't wonder at it. But Miss Trubb can't or won't help herself, so someone has to do it for her.'

'Exactly.' Mr Meadows smiled so kindly that Mavis began to be a little ashamed of Reg's vehemence. 'Surely now that she is in such excellent hands, in the right sort of hospital . . . ?'

'That's just it,' Reg interrupted, rudely. 'We don't think she is. In the right place, I mean. We think she's a hundred per cent sane. We always have.'

Mr Meadows's face hardened. Then he covered his eyes with one hand, and sighed heavily.

'I need not tell you of my early association with the Clements family,' he began. 'I am sure you have gone into it during your – shall we call it – self-imposed research. But I should like you to remember my close friendship with Helen, up to the time she – betrayed it. I have always preferred to consider that betrayal and all that followed as the product of an unstable temperament, culminating in an act of pure madness.'

Reg felt slightly sick. There was venom behind the rolling jargon speech, venom and wounded vanity. He exchanged a quick look with Mavis, and was relieved to see in her eyes the same disgust he was feeling.

'As an explanation it makes the whole thing more respectable, I agree,' he said, roughly. 'The point is, it can't be true.'

He looked at Colin in desperation.

'I'm sorry, sir,' he said, trying at last not to antagonize the visitor, but win him to his own view, 'but we simply don't understand why you didn't get at the father of the child at the time. Why did you let there be all that mystery? If you were as interested in Helen as you say you were.'

Mr Meadows drew himself up.

'I did not come here to discuss my private affairs,' he said. 'But I can set your minds at rest on some points, at least. Helen left Weyford without giving me any explanation of her reasons for doing so. Without even telling me in advance. She wrote to me occasionally from Conington. In fact, I thought she wanted to break off our friendship and was afraid to do it openly. Then I heard from her sister, whom I had seen very occasionally in Weyford during the same period, that Helen had just had a baby. I was very deeply shocked.'

It sounded natural enough, Reg thought. An ordinary story, but not the sort of thing you'd expect from Miss Trubb.

'It must have been awful for you,' said Mavis, warmly. She was all sympathy for his situation.

Mr Meadows looked grateful.

'It was never known in Weyford until after old Mr Clements's death,' he said. 'We managed to keep it from him. His health was already failing, though the end came unexpectedly. It would have killed him. Helen was always his favourite. Though, after she left, Frances did gradually take her place.'

There was a complacent note in his voice as he said this. Reg remembered the clerk's complete success, his inheritance through his wife of the entire business. A faint chill crept over him as he thought of these things.

'Nothing was known,' went on Mr Meadows, 'until the death of the child and Helen's arrest and trial. I had only just been invalided out of the Army, after months in hospital. My wife was at Weyford, looking after our own little boy. It was a very very terrible time for us. Frances has never quite got over it.'

'It would be hard to get over,' said Reg, 'because there was always the doubt, as the Home Secretary said, when he reprieved her.'

'There was no doubt in *our* minds,' said Colin Meadows, icily. 'No doubt at all, I'm afraid.'

The conversation languished. The young couple could not

agree to end their interest in Miss Trubb, nor their inquiries into her past.

'But, as you said, it's practically out of our hands now,' Mavis assured Colin, as they saw him into his car at their garden gate. 'What with the police taking an interest at last, and Mr Warrington-Reeve going to town over it. And the solicitor is helping him. I expect you know Mr Coke, don't you?'

'Oh, yes,' answered Mr Meadows. 'I know Coke quite well.'

CHAPTER 11

'Frankly, we weren't much taken with Mr Meadows's manner,' Reg told Warrington-Reeve, the next time they met.

They were sitting in the barrister's room in chambers. The leaves had fallen now from the trees, and their dark trunks rose out of a thin mist that lay over the grass, pale grey against the dusk. The lights were on in the room. It occurred to Reg, remembering his first visit in early autumn, that some considerable time had passed since then. Two months, in fact.

'We haven't done all that much, have we? So far?' he said.

Warrington-Reeve smiled.

'I don't agree. I think you and your wife have done a great deal. I wish there had been people like you on the job sixteen years ago.'

'You wouldn't have taken our word for it, then,' said Reg.

'Perhaps not. Tell me more about Meadows.'

'He tried to pull the big boss over me. Nothing doing. I think he's scared about the whole business.'

'Why should he be?'

'Mainly in case he gets adverse publicity. You could see he was dead set on keeping the past down. I suppose now he's got to his present position in Weyford – he's a town coun-cillor, I believe – he'll avoid any sort of scandal at all costs.'

'That would be a strong motive with some people. You consider him ultra-respectable, ultra-conventional?'

'That's right.'

'Nothing more? Always remembering his wife may have been the mother of that baby?'

'Mavis thinks, if she had, she'd be the last to tell him. She'd keep it from him at all costs.'

'That would be consistent, wouldn't it, with her foisting it off on Helen?'

'She wasn't married to him, then.'

'No, but she may have intended to be.'

'I see what you mean.'

Warrington-Reeve took over the argument.

'I was not much impressed with the artist friend of Mrs Meadows's youth. He can paint, certainly. A spoiled genius, perhaps. But a thoroughly nasty type. On the other hand, I think he knows something, either about Frances, or her other boy friends. Perhaps it's the same thing. He was startled when I mentioned the name of Coke. Thought I meant the solicitor's cousin. So I decided to take Stephen Coke into our confidence over this man. It was not easy, until I found out, very discreetly, that they were scarcely on speaking terms now, though their wives are still friendly.'

'Leslie Coke is not likely to know what we're up to, then? I bet he's another that would do anything to keep the past walled up.'

'I gathered from Stephen that Leslie is wholly preoccupied with the rocky state of his own business. His accountancy has been unconventional, I gathered. Stephen apparently warned him some years ago to be more careful, but he persisted in his gambles and odd practices, so he washed his hands of him. Unfortunately, and this again Stephen deplored, his wife is more than ever attached to Mrs Leslie, and the two spend a great deal of time together, chiefly at Stephen's house.'

'Does he tell his wife about his business?'

'Nothing to do with his clients, of course. But he had discussed Miss Trubb's recent history with her. After all, these women all went to the same school at Weyford when they were children.'

'And she'll have passed that on to Leslie's wife, you mean? So he'll most likely know as much as we do?'

'Unfortunately, up to the present time, yes.'

'Have you seen Leslie himself?'

Warrington-Reeve nodded.

'I have. A very smooth character. You'd never suspect he fancied himself as a budding artist at one time. He says he still sketches, mostly in the countryside round Weyford. He considers it a good relaxation. Like Churchill, he said, putting in an apologetic laugh, that wouldn't deceive a saint. I got nothing out of him at all. Not a sausage.'

'But we do know he was a special friend of Frances Meadows?'

'During the time they were both at the art school. His wife was there too, for a bit, and knows Frances quite well. But on the whole neither of the Coke families are particular friends of the Meadows now.'

Reg looked rather downcast.

'It doesn't get us much further, does it?' he said. 'Two chaps who might have been the father of that child, supposing it was Frances's, not Helen's. A fair certainty Frances was acting wild and silly at that time. But that being so, and seeing she married him later, why not Colin Meadows?'

'In that case he'd have known, and wouldn't they have taken the child to live with them?'

'He wouldn't. It'd have spoiled his chances with old man Clements. He told us, and I'll swear he was speaking the truth, that they kept the news of that child's birth from the old boy until he died. Meadows would never have got his mitts on the business, if Mr Clements had known he'd seduced his daughter.'

'Either of his daughters,' said Warrington-Reeve.

They looked gravely at one another.

'Meadows was thought to be fond of Helen,' went on the barrister. 'Suppose he fathered the child on her. He was angry and frightened for his career and would do nothing to help her. So she left home and suffered in silence and disillusion. A year later he marries her sister. More disillusion. Her father dies, disinheriting her. In a fit of despair she kills the child. Isn't that a consistent story?'

'Meadows would be capable of it,' answered Reg. 'From what we saw of him. And Miss Trubb might act like that: all the first part. But she'd never kill a child.'

It was growing automatic, that sentence, he thought. But he still believed in it.

Warrington-Reeve frowned. His young friend was beginning to be a bore, in his monotonous and fanatical support of Miss Trubb.

'It is clear to me,' he said, pompously, 'that we know far too little about Helen Clements. I thought so at the time of the trial, and I still think so. The trouble then was the upheaval of the war. Now it should be easier. I'll get on to Coke again and see if he can't produce some intimate friends of Helen's this time.'

'You'd better warn him not to tell his wife what he's doing,' said Reg.

'Quite so. I'll impress on him that we want to avoid local gossip and that in any case it would not be fair to involve an old friend of Helen's. It might be a good thing if you and your wife took over, supposing we find someone suitable. It would look less formal, and that sort of thing. I'm afraid I did rather scare poor Raymond Thorne. Though I expect he is usually too drunk these days to remember very much of what goes on in his life.'

The result of this interview arrived, in the shape of two letters to Reg, one from Warrington-Reeve, explaining that Mr Coke had put him in touch with some very old friends of Miss Trubb, and the other from these friends, a farmer and his wife, who lived about five miles from Weyford.

'Chap called Bradley,' said Reg, handing the letter over to Mavis. 'Says they'd be pleased to have us call.'

A paper fell to the floor as he spoke. He stooped to pick it up.

'What's that?' Mavis asked.

Reg shook the envelope he still held in his hand.

'Must have been in with the letter. It's a sketch map of how to get to their place. They seem quite keen to have us, don't they?'

Mavis, who had now read the short letter, handed it back.

'He doesn't say much, does he?'

'What would you expect? He's never heard of us till now. What there is sounds all right. Pleased to hear we take a sympathetic interest in Helen Clements. Doesn't call her Trubb, you notice.'

'Yes, I saw that. We'll go down, won't we? They won't mind Joy going with us? She's a bit fretty with her teeth this week – '

'He says Sunday next. We ought to make it, if we can.'

So it was settled. Mavis sent a card to confirm their intended visit, and Reg put the sketch map in his wallet to be sure of taking it with him. His own road map of the district did not show Stowe Farm, which lay in a part of the Wey valley where the stream moved slowly through marshy land, dividing into several backwaters, some of which joined the main river again lower down. As Mr Bradley explained in his letter, their farm could be reached in several ways, as it stood on higher ground at one edge of the valley. Their best and quickest route lay off the Portsmouth Road, by a narrow lane, which could easily be missed, as it was not well sign-posted. Hence the sketch map.

Reg and Mavis found this was only too true. They made one mistake, ending in a group of new houses, and had to go back to the main road and try again. But it was a fine November day, with a clear sky, and a low sun that made its warmth felt through the windows of the car, though there was a nip in the air outside. At the next attempt they turned off the Portsmouth Road with renewed confidence. The side road they took this time was one on Reg's road map, as well as on the sketch plan. But as they proceeded along this lane, with high hedges obscuring the view and frequent small houses, unnamed and unnumbered, appearing on either side in no sort of order or arrangement, they began to wonder how they would ever find the right turning from it.

'Any one of these private drives could be it,' said Reg, backing out of the third they had attempted. 'I've lost count. I suppose we haven't passed a real side road at all yet?'

'It says go through Tilbey as far as the Hen and Chicken. Then cross two bridges and then consult the map for the turning off to the left.'

'Tilbey was where we left the Portsmouth Road. Is all this still Tilbey? The houses don't seem to end.'

'It must be. Anyway, we haven't passed the Hen and Chicken. Oh, there it is! On the right, standing back.'

'It would be. What d'you say we stop off for a quick one

and get a bit more information? That sketch map looks dicey to me.'

'Oh, Reg, we can't! We're late already, and Joy'd wake up and start creating. And they'd be sure to hear of it, later.'

'Is it a crime to have a drink?'

'Of course not. But there isn't time.'

Reg, who had slowed down the car, pressed his foot on the throttle, and they shot on their way.

'Don't go too fast,' said Mavis. 'I've got to count the turnings from now on.'

'No pleasing you, is there?' said Reg, irritably.

'Here we are – I think.'

They had crossed two bridges, according to instructions. Reg had counted them. The road was winding across a curious flat plain, with marshy fields lying well below its level, bordered by untidy hedges near the road and divided by broad dykes filled with stagnant water. A strong river smell came into the car, as Mavis wound the window down to put her head out. While Reg slowed down and took the car out of gear they heard the rustle and tinkle of water on each side. Mavis pointed out a narrow lane which left the road and seemed to go sharply downhill into the surrounding fields.

'The farm is on high ground not far from the river,' Reg objected.

'Well, there's no harm in going down and then up again,' Mavis answered. 'Look for yourself, if you don't believe me. We've got another bridge to cross. It's down here, I expect, and the farm up the far side.'

'O.K., O.K. I'll try it. We can only come back if it's wrong. What does the sign-post say?'

The sign-post, unlike others they had passed, giving the names of several villages, bore only one word: Woking.

'Bloody lot of use!' grumbled Reg. 'Still, it goes somewhere. We might as well try it.'

The lane was very narrow indeed, with a belt of willow trees on the left. But the surface was fair, and knowing they were late, Reg pressed on, taking the next corner rather faster than he intended.

Mavis's scream and the squeal of his tyres came almost

together. For the corner led to a scene and a situation as frightening as it was unexpected.

There were no trees here, no hedges, only a short stretch of grass on either side of the road, which led down steeply to where a bridge should have been. But there was no bridge, only a rough wooden plank supported on two rickety trestles, and carrying a red flag at the centre. Beyond that was the bank and beyond that the Wey, flowing swiftly past in a muddy stream, swollen by recent rain.

All this would have been enough in itself to startle them, to make Mavis scream in terror and Reg swear roughly and stamp on his brakes and swing the car round on to the grass, bringing it violently to a standstill. But there was more. A motor-cycle lay on its side at the very edge of the river, and beside it lay the body of a man.

Reg was out of the car before it had stopped rocking. He noticed the long skid marks the motor-bike had made. Obviously this driver, too, had tried to stop suddenly when he saw the bridge was down. But had not been able to stay on his machine.

Reg knelt beside him, but he knew he was dead. Dead, and already stiff, but not quite cold. His crash helmet had rolled off, the strap broken; a terrible and bloody wound disfigured his right temple and cheek.

Reg looked at the motor-cycle and back at the man. From the way the bike was laying and the skid marks in the road and on the grass, the man must have fallen to his left. You would expect the main injury to be at the point of contact, Reg thought. Well, there might be something worse the other side. There was a lot of blood on the ground. But this injury, he saw, would certainly be fatal.

'He's dead, isn't he?' Mavis's voice cut into his thoughts.

'Yes, darling. Don't look. Go back to the car. Is Joy all right?'

'She's still asleep, believe it or not.' Mavis's voice was shaky. 'I can't help looking. How did it happen?'

'That's just it. Look, could you help me?'

'How?'

'Push that shoulder and roll him over a bit. I want to see where he hit the ground.'

109

She gathered up her courage and did as Reg wanted.

'O.K.,' he said. 'Let him down again, gently.'

He got up and stood looking at the crumpled form at his feet.

'What beats me,' he said, in a puzzled voice, 'is how he got that blow on the *right* side of his head. There's enough on the *left* side to knock him out, I'd think. He may have somersaulted, but even then – it's all soft grass here. No rocks or anything. The skid suggests he was still on the machine when it left the road. I don't understand it.'

'There's something I don't understand!' cried Mavis indignantly. She was recovering, and looking about her. The gurgling river was horribly near. If it hadn't been for the poor devil lying there, they would almost certainly have been into it. She and Reg had both seen the bike first, before they realized the bridge had gone.

'That bridge,' she said. 'It hasn't fallen in by accident or been washed away by a flood or anything. You can see they're working on it. They're taking it down on purpose. Besides, there's a danger sign.'

'A damned useless one,' said Reg.

'*He* saved our lives,' said Mavis, feeling sick. She had begun to feel the later effects of the shock. She shivered and her teeth were chattering.

'Go back to the car, darling and sit down.'

'We must get help. The police.'

'I know. We will. I just want to find out who he is – if I can.'

'You mustn't touch him! It isn't our business! Leave it all to the police.'

'Oh, I will. Don't you worry.'

He knelt beside the dead man and slipped his hand very carefully into the available pockets, one by one. He was lucky. In the outer pocket of the man's padded jacket he found an envelope addressed to 'Leslie Coke. Accountant.' Inside there was a letter from an address that finished, 'Nr. Woking.' Reg put the letter back where he found it and walked over to the car.

'The man you think saved our lives was Leslie Coke,' he told Mavis. 'Slim Leslie, who apparently was going to square

one of his unfortunate and irate clients. So now we'll go back
to the Hen and Chicken, and have that drink you were not
so keen on. And I'll tell the police and we'll get on to the
farm, too.'

'And Mr Coke, hadn't we better?'

'I wonder. He didn't like his cousin.'

Reg turned the car and drove slowly back along the narrow
lane, and waited very carefully before moving out on to the
wider one.

'What I don't understand,' he said, 'is why Mr Bradley
directed us down that lane when the bridge is out of
commission. He must have known, and it can't be the only
approach to his farm. He said you could get there from
several directions. So why choose this one?'

'They may have started on the bridge after he wrote.'

'They haven't done all that inside a week.'

'He'd expect us to see that notice,' Mavis said, as Reg
moved on.

'It wasn't a notice, only a red flag on a pole.'

'No. I mean that notice.'

She was turning round and pointing.

'*What!*'

Reg drew into the side of the road, and they both jumped
out of the car, looking back at the entrance to the narrow
lane. A white board stood there, at the side, and on it in large
black letters was written, 'Road Closed'.

'It wasn't there before! I swear it wasn't!' Reg cried,
furiously.

'I didn't see it. It wasn't my side, then. I was studying the
map. And the sign-post.'

'It wasn't there, I tell you!'

'But it is, now,' said Mavis, slowly.

CHAPTER 12

Reg rang up the Weyford police, and was told to wait at the Hen and Chicken until they arrived. He then rang up Mr Bradley. The farmer was shocked to hear his news, and even more horrified to learn that his sketch map had been so misleading. He could not understand this at all. He remembered distinctly putting a line across the road in question, and arrows passing it and pointing down the next turning but one on the same side.

Reg had looked at the map so often that he could have drawn it himself from memory without hesitation. He realized at once, when Mr Bradley began to argue, that the paper he had received could not be the one posted by the farmer. Here was another strange occurrence, which the police would have to know about. He decided not to discuss it with Bradley just then.

'I'm stuck here, I'm afraid,' he said. 'Got to wait for the coppers. It'll be too late to come on to you then, I expect. We thought of having lunch here at the pub.'

There was a silence. Then a woman's voice said, 'This is Mrs Bradley speaking. I quite understand, Mr Holmes. I'm so sorry you have had all this upset. But if you are not too tired when the police have finished, and would still like to see us, we shall have tea ready for you about half-past four.'

'That's very good of you, Mrs Bradley. I'm very sorry to have caused all this inconvenience.'

'It isn't your fault at all. Perhaps it was a good thing. People don't go near that bridge at present. We natives know it's down, and the day trippers see the Road Closed notice.'

She added, slowly, 'I'm still wondering how you came to miss it.'

'I'll tell you when we meet,' said Reg, and rang off.

The Hen and Chicken did not normally serve meals, as the landlord explained several times. But still, Sunday hours were always difficult, and they'd had this shock, and the child must be famished, so the wife would knock up something for them.

The 'something' proved to be a cut off the family joint, with a generous helping of vegetables from the garden behind the pub.

'I bet we couldn't have done better at Stowe Farm itself,' Reg told the landlord, who came in person to change their plates.

'That where you were going?'

'We're going on to tea. Excuse me – ' He got up hurriedly, for he had seen from the window of the saloon bar, where they were eating, a black car with a uniformed figure at the wheel.

'I'll talk to them,' he said to Mavis. 'You carry on with your dinner.'

'So you drove down there?' asked the local detective-sergeant, getting out of the police car, followed by Reg.

'Yes. That notice was not in the middle of the road, then. There was no notice visible till we came back into this road, and then it was propped up at the side. It must have been put back in the middle during the last twenty minutes.'

'I see. You say you drove into the turning and later drove back.'

'That's right.'

Sergeant Willis was used to dealing with road accidents. He had developed them as a speciality. So he set about inspecting the various tracks in the soft surface of the lane with great interest and loving care.

'You certainly didn't have a notice in the middle of the lane when you went in,' he said, nodding vigorously. 'Nor when you came out. But the bike took the extreme verge. It might have gone round a notice. Can't say for certain.'

'Don't you want to see the body?' asked Reg, considerably

113

shocked by the other's deliberate and pointless antics, as he considered them.

Sergeant Willis, rather red in the face from marking off various sections of track for further study, stood up, winding in his tape.

'All in good time,' he said. 'You reported him stiff, so you couldn't be wrong about his death, and nothing can be done for him. We shall have the ambulance here shortly, and the doctor and others, and I don't want them messing up this end before we've recorded it. You're right about the notice, anyway. You couldn't very well have driven straight through it both ways and left it standing.'

He grinned cheerfully, but Reg was not amused. He wanted to get back to Mavis and his interrupted lunch.

'What's more,' he snapped, 'it must have been deliberately hidden. And that ties with the instructions I got from Mr Bradley how to reach his place, Stowe Farm.'

'Mr *Bradley?*' asked Willis, shocked out of his calm deliberation. He snatched the misleading map from Reg's hand. 'You say he sent you this?'

'It came in his letter. Apparently he thinks he sent a different one.'

'You've spoken to him about it?'

'On the phone.'

'Mind if I keep it? I'll be taking it up with Mr Bradley.'

Reg nodded. He preferred to think the police would sort it out with the farmer. It would save any argument. He didn't want to get across a stranger at the start of their acquaintance. He wanted to learn a few things about Miss Trubb.

Sergeant Willis walked on down the lane. Reg was surprized how much further it seemed on foot than in the car. When they turned into the open space before the river the sergeant hurried forward. He stood staring down at the twisted body on the grass.

'Well!' Reg heard him say, as he drew near. 'Well, well, well!'

'You recognize him, then?' Reg said.

'Yes. Do you?'

'No.'

This was true, and Reg was not going to explain his former

curiosity, nor its result. But he saw no harm in putting forward his doubt about the manner of the man's death.

'I didn't try to move him,' he said. 'Beyond what was necessary to make sure he was dead. But I don't see why that bash on his head is this side. It ought to be underneath.'

'It ought not to be there at all,' said Sergeant Willis.

There were voices in the lane, and some men came round the corner. Willis went over to them and began to talk rapidly in tones too low for Reg to hear. When he had finished the sergeant beckoned to him.

'These chaps will get on with it now,' he said. 'I want to get back to the pub and phone. Then I'll take your statement briefly and that will be all for the present. You understand you'll have to attend the inquest in due course. Did you say you were going on to Stowe Farm?'

'Yes.'

'And back to London this evening?'

'That's right.'

'Are you friends of the Bradleys?'

'No. But I don't know what that has to do with this accident.'

Sergeant Willis frowned, and Reg rushed in to defend himself.

'Doesn't look much like knowing them, to take a wrong turn to their place, does it? Nor for him to have sent a map, even if it was misleading.'

'It has only been a wrong turn since they started on that bridge, about three weeks ago.'

'I'm glad to know how long, because his letter and the map sent to me only a few *days* ago. It looks very much as if someone wanted to stop me talking to Mr Bradley. Or perhaps only stop – that man – talking ever again.'

'Look,' said Sergeant Willis. 'You've got eyes in your head and a gift of the gab. Suppose you use the first and give the second a rest. In your own interests, strictly. I mean it for your own good, mind you.'

Reg saw the wisdom of this, though he resented it.

'O.K.,' he said. 'And what do I do if I see anything else of interest? Keep it to myself?'

'We'll be seeing you again,' said Willis, pleasantly. 'Keep it till then.'

Reg went into the Hen and Chicken to find his family, and Sergeant Willis went into the public call box outside the little pub. His local Superintendent answered.

'Leslie Coke is dead, down by the river, beyond Tilbey,' Willis reported. 'He either skidded or was tripped off his motor-bike, just short of the water. I think he was meant to go into it, but this failed, so he got an almightly clout on the side of the head, as he lay on the ground. It looks as if his murky past has caught up with him.'

As soon as the suspicion of foul play was established, the full resources of the Weyford C.I.D. came into play. And very soon the range of inquiry was widened.

A pathologist from the Home Office was summoned immediately to a consultation with the local man in examining the body, and police in a small motor launch dragged the swollen Wey for any blunt object that might have dealt the fatal blow. Sergeant Willis, with his superior, Inspector Frost, went to the house of the dead man's cousin.

Mr Coke was prepared for the visit.

'Leslie's wife rang us up as soon as she knew,' he explained. 'My wife is with her now. How can I help you?'

Inspector Frost explained the curious nature of the dead man's injuries.

'By themselves, they need explaining, but are not conclusive,' he went on. 'The odd thing is why he went down that lane at all. He must have known – everyone knows – that the bridge is under reconstruction.'

'He may have wanted to paint the landscape. He was fond of sketching and often went out to do it on Sunday morning.'

'Yes. There were sketching materials on the carrier of the bike. But it did look as if he was driving down fast, and tried to stop suddenly. The skid marks suggest it. Going that way was consistent with a letter in his pocket. You may as well see it. That address could best be reached by the lane. It was the shortest, most direct route. There was trouble coming from that quarter, as you see. He may have been on his way to stave it off.'

Mr Coke read the letter with a pained expression. He foresaw a great deal of 'trouble', as the Inspector called it, before his cousin's dubious affairs subsided into the grave with him and were decently forgotten.

'You may be right,' he said. 'And Leslie may have thought the work on the bridge was finished. But surely, if it wasn't, the road would still be closed?'

'That's just it,' said Inspector Frost. 'We have definite evidence the notice was moved, at any rate shortly after Mr Coke's death, and almost certainly before. Tell him, Willis.'

So Sergeant Willis went on with an account of the Holmes' experience, and at this point Mr Coke's horrifed reaction startled both the police officers.

'But this is dreadful!' Mr Coke explained. 'I know these young people. They have been engaged in activities they had no right to undertake. You had better hear the full story.'

The full story meant nothing to Sergeant Willis, but it recalled to Inspector Frost his first years in the Weyford Force, and reminded him, too, of the recent visit to Weyford of Inspector Brown from South London. At the end of it he thanked Mr Coke and said he must get back to the Station.

'Have they gone back to town?' Mr Coke asked at the front door of his house. 'I mean Reg and Mavis Holmes?'

'Probably, by now. They were going up to Stowe Farm this afternoon.'

'I feel rather to blame,' Mr Coke said, nervously. 'I put them in touch with the Bradleys. After asking Bob's permission, of course. His wife was such a close friend of Helen's in the old days. They were looking for the farm, I suppose? And there was no notice, did you say? Surely that is very dangerous?'

'There was no notice when they went into the lane, but they saw it by the side when they came out, after finding the body. They reported to us at once from the Hen and Chicken. When we went along, the notice was back in its proper place at the middle of the turning into the lane.'

Mr Coke's face was very pale.

'How dreadful!' he said again, in a low voice. 'It does sound quite deliberate. But was it meant for Leslie or the Holmeses?'

'That's one of the things we've got to find out,' said Inspector Frost.

As they got back into the police car he said to the driver, 'Drop me at the Station and go on to Stowe Farm. See if you can get any sense on this sketch map, Ted,' he went on, turning to Willis. 'Follow up anything you do find. That couple from London should be gone by now. Don't take up the Trubb angle. I'm getting on to that myself. I don't like this business, and that's a fact. Too many bloody angles. Anyway, see what you can get out of Bradley.'

Inspector Frost reported the whole affair to the Chief Constable, who told him to concentrate on the death of Leslie Coke. The primary report from the two pathologists, and another from a motoring expert, suggested that Coke could not have died from falling off his machine. There was evidence that he had struck the ground on his left side, taking the brunt of it on the point of his left shoulder. The collar bone and the neck of the humerus were broken, and there were cracks in the scapula. He had remained in the position in which he fell. Marks in the ground and on his clothing proved this. The savage blow to the right temple must have been delivered as he lay helpless. He had clearly been murdered.

This was more important, the Chief Constable pointed out, than a problematical scheme to stop the Holmes couple's inquiries by making them drive into the river. In any case the two things were not connected.

Inspector Frost did not agree, but he refrained from saying so. He decided to wait for Sergeant Willis's report. This came in late that evening.

'Bradley swears the map I showed him, the one young Holmes gave me, is not the one he made and put in with his letter. His one showed the lane with a thick bar across it to mark its being closed.'

'Then how did the other map get into the letter?'

'That's just it. Bradley says he felt a bit dubious about seeing the Holmeses and starting up anything about Miss Trubb without warning her sister. So he asked Mrs Meadows and her husband over to discuss it and showed them his letter before putting it in the envelope. They said they didn't mind as the poor woman was mental and in hospital, and nothing could be done for her, as these young friends of hers would soon find out. The upshot of this visit was that Bradley gave the letter, fastened up by now, with the map inside, to Colin Meadows to post.'

'You went to see the Meadows after that, I take it?'

'Yes. Incidentally the Holmeses had been there already, about the same thing. He was out when I called, but she was in. She said they both forgot the letter that day, but her husband found it in his pocket the next morning. Being in a hurry to get on to business he gave it to her. She spent the morning in her garden, there being a lot to do clearing up before the winter. She didn't go out. Mrs Leslie Coke came to see her in the afternoon, and she gave her the letter to post when she left.'

'Did she post it?'

'Yes. I got on to her after I left Mrs Meadows. I didn't like to press her too much. She can't remember if it was that day or the following morning.'

'Can't *remember*?'

'She kept saying what had it got to do with Leslie's death, and to leave her alone.'

'O.K. You've got all the dates?'

'Bar the postmark on the envelope. Let's hope Holmes kept it. I expect he did. He seemed intelligent. We shall have to see that young man again. Mrs Meadows wasn't too pleased with him coming on to them from the Bradleys like that. She said her husband hadn't been too pleased, either. She thought it was time they left off asking questions about Miss Trubb.'

'Oh, that!' said Inspector Frost. 'One-track mind, that young man!'

Miss Trubb slipped in through the hospital gate while her friend Hilda engaged the porter in conversation, filling up the space before his lodge with her enormous bulk. Hilda had been out on parole. Miss Trubb's parole had been stopped since the night she came in too late.

She knew why it had been stopped. They did not believe her when she told them the truth about Joy. They said why didn't she wait with the child until her mother came back?

Or take her straight to her home and wait there? Where had she been? What had she really intended to do to Joy?

She could not answer any of these questions. The answers would sound even stranger than her unexplained actions. She could not tell anyone that she had seen the enemy again, lurking in the bushes of that public garden. That she had watched the enemy go away, and had almost rushed out to tell Mavis to take Joy home at once and never come there again. But she had restrained herself, until she saw little Joy all alone on her rug, and had been overwhelmed by an instinct to save her immediately from the lurking threat. And after that she had walked about, often avoiding the police, terrified of what she had done, and the interpretation that would be put on it. Until at last, with night falling, she had forced herself to go back to Twenty-six Sandfields Avenue, and suffer the consequences of her impulse.

She had told the truth, except about the enemy, and they did not believe her, or thought it merely showed a more severe mental change. She did not mind that. She was safer in the hospital than outside it. But she had to be free to go out and in. She had to know that Reg and Mavis and Joy were safe and well. Particularly Joy.

So she had appealed to Hilda for help, and the poor anxious creature, never quite sure of herself, but always suspicious of authority, had taken a sly pleasure in covering her surreptitious entrances and exits. There was very little Miss Trubb did not know about evasion after fifteen years of practice. The porters on the gate were child's play to warders, and were men, which made all kinds of differences.

On this Sunday evening Miss Trubb said good night and thank you to her friend, Hilda, and made her way to her own villa.

'We've missed you all afternoon,' said the nurse in charge, later.

'It was fine, Nurse. I like the fresh air.'

'You've been out again, haven't you?'

Miss Trubb did not answer.

'I shall have to report it.'

Miss Trubb turned her mind away from Nurse's threats and appeals. It was quite easy. You dropped the shutter between yourself and the world outside, when that world became unendurable. She had things to think about, besides. And other people, not only Reg and Mavis. There was Raymond Thorne, who had remembered her from the old days in spite of the change in her. Had she really changed less than he? She had not recognized him until he faced her squarely that day, that dreadful day, greeting her by the name she never used. Was it he, perhaps, who had betrayed her? He was dangerous, but, nevertheless, she had been to look for him now, at the, address he had given her.

He was not surprised, seemingly. He was quite affable, and suggested they should go for a walk together. So they had taken a bus and then walked on Wimbledon Common, and he had told her, still in the same friendly manner, the most terrible, heartrending, impossible things. She had been quite carried away by rage and grief. So she had left him, and gone home again to the hospital, alone.

Sitting by herself in a corner of the lounge at the villa, Miss Trubb shivered. You could drop the shutter, but the real world pressed hard on the outside of it, trying to get in, trying to destroy her. There was nothing more she could do but wait for that ultimate attack and the long deferred, bitterly contested, end.

CHAPTER 13

With fresh directions, and after a conference with the land-lord of the Hen and Chicken, Reg had no difficulty in finding Stowe Farm. He was met at the gate of the farmhouse garden by Mr Bradley himself.

'You've had a nasty experience,' the latter said, when they had introduced themselves.

'It was horrible,' said Mavis. 'That poor man!'

Mr Bradley took them indoors and in a few minutes Mrs Bradley had the tea ready. Neither Reg nor Mavis had much appetite, as it was not very long since their late lunch, and the events of the morning were not such as to promote hearty eating. But the hot drink was a comfort, and something to occupy them during their rather difficult conversation.

Reg apologized again for bothering them with his inquiries and for raising the painful subject of Miss Trubb, whom perhaps they no longer wanted to regard as a friend.

'It wasn't us that made the break,' Mrs Bradley protested. 'We were terribly shocked, and very sorry for her, naturally. But we were ready to do all we could. Only she insisted on cutting herself off entirely. She was always very thorough in everything she did. Right from a girl, wasn't she, Bob?'

'Yes. It was hard to us to believe any of her story, from the time she left Weyford. It wasn't a bit like Helen. But I must admit she'd altered in the years since her mother died. We knew her as kids, you understand. Helen was always the leader at school, responsible, good ideas and all that. And always laughing and happy. Nothing was too much trouble for her. Nothing scared her. But she wasn't reckless or silly. That was Frances, more.'

'Frances was just the opposite of Helen,' said Mrs Bradley. 'I don't mean to say she was actively naughty as a child. Butter wouldn't melt in her mouth when there was anything she wanted. But underneath she was very wilful. Her mother never knew how to manage her. She couldn't trust her, she used to tell my mother. Helen couldn't manage her either, though she tried hard enough.'

'Too hard,' said Mr Bradley. 'Many's the time we told her to let Frances go her own way. But she kept on trying to look after her, and train her. You see, Mrs Clements made Helen swear a solemn oath to care for Frances. In spite of her sly ways Mrs Clements cared more for her than for Helen.'

'That's often the way, isn't it?' said Mavis, wisely. 'The younger one or the pretty one gets spoiled.'

'Mrs Clements didn't exactly spoil her,' answered Mrs Bradley. 'But she certainly admired her looks. She hoped she'd settle down and marry a sensible man who'd keep her in order.'

'Which is what she did,' said Mr Bradley, 'though her poor mother didn't live to see it.'

'Colin Meadows may be sensible,' said Mrs Bradley, 'but I shouldn't think he'd make a good husband. Always out for himself, and always has been.'

'The wife has never forgiven him for how he treated Helen,' explained Mr Bradley.

'Was he actually engaged to her?' Reg asked.

'Not officially,' answered Mrs Bradley. 'It was taken for granted, though. I know for a fact when she left home so suddenly she wrote to him, saying she would tell him why later, but could not do so at present. In the letter she left for her father she simply said she had gone to do war work, and had not warned him in order to avoid an argument when her mind was made up. She knew him well, of course. As obstinate as she was herself. And what does Colin do? Never sent her a line, never went to find her and make her say why she'd gone. Just ignored her from then on, sucked up to the old man on his home leaves, and began to make a dead set at Frances. Right away.'

'But not for long,' put in Mr Bradley. 'He was sent up north in the middle of April and Frances was away permanently, from about the same time. But they must have been corresponding because by the end of the summer, when Frances went into the W.A.A.F., they were known to be sweet on each other.'

'When did you first hear that Helen had got a child?' Mavis asked.

'Oh, we knew about that time. It was Frances told us.'

'Not Helen herself?'

'Not she. I told you, after that first letter we never heard from her again. It hurt me very badly that she didn't confide in me,' said Mrs Bradley. 'It was so unlike her, and we had been such friends.'

'Didn't you go to see her?'

'I didn't know where she was for over two years. Frances wouldn't tell me for a long time. Said Helen had sworn her to secrecy. I didn't know whether to believe her or not. She told me some time after she married Colin. After her own child was born. Naturally I went up to Conington at once and found Helen and the child.'

Mrs Bradley's eyes filled with tears.

'We were properly upset, both of us,' said the farmer gruffly. 'The whole thing was totally unexpected. Helen Clements was the last girl on earth I'd have expected it of. Thinking it all over I began to wonder if it was Colin that let her down. We'd never heard of anyone else she went about with. That's in strict confidence, mind. He's the sort of chap that'd take an action for slander like a shot, if he saw any cash in it. Publicity wouldn't affect him.'

'We've always wondered about that,' said Reg, 'in the intervals of wondering if Miss Trubb had the child at all. We thought it might really have belonged to Frances – Mrs Meadows, I mean. That was why we wanted to see you. You certainly confirm what we know about her behaviour at the art school.'

The Bradleys exchanged glances. Clearly they had always had doubts themselves.

'I begged Helen to tell me the truth that one time I saw her,' Mrs Bradley went on. 'She went so far as to say it wasn't hers, but she had to pass it off as hers to get the rations and that. I didn't understand what she meant, but it came out later at the trial about the birth certificate and the identity cards and so on. She wouldn't tell me whose it was, though. And when I got home, I said to Bob that Helen was too sensible and truthful and honest to go to such lengths for anyone except Frances, because she'd sworn to her dying mother to look after her.'

'Frances knew that, too, I expect,' said Mavis.

'Knew it and traded on it,' agreed Mrs Bradley, with indignation. 'Often and often, to my certain knowledge, Helen got her out of scrapes, both at school and at the art college.'

'Would Frances have gone to the length of letting her own sister take all that blame?'

'She might.'

'But later, would she have let Helen go to trial on the charge of murdering her own child, if it was not hers? I mean, if it was Frances's?'

'The child was dead, whoever bore it. Frances thought the crime was committed by her sister. She brought that out in the trial. She was a witness for the prosecution,' Reg reminded them.

'Perhaps if it was true, she'd want Helen convicted.'

'If it was hers, she never cared twopence for it,' said Mrs Bradley. 'But Helen did. I saw that when I was with her for those few hours at Conington.'

Mavis shook her head.

'We *know* how she feels about children,' she said. 'That's why we're here. Why did she let herself be accused and not defend herself? She might have been hanged. Was that all for Frances?'

'It could have been only for Frances, according to Mrs Bradley, here,' said Reg, slowly. 'And you see what that means, don't you?' He looked round at all of the others. The Bradleys stared at him, growing horror in their eyes. 'It could only have been because she *knew* Frances was the real murderess, and that she'd killed her own child.'

None of them spoke. After a few seconds Reg went on.

'What I can't understand,' he said, 'is why the defence never checked on Mrs Meadows at the time of the trial. There was her own evidence, of course, of where she had been during the time supposed to be occupied by Miss Trubb's pregnancy. But there was no corroboration from employers or fellow workers or anyone.'

'It wasn't Frances they were trying for murder,' said Mr Bradley. 'It was the murder that mattered. If Helen didn't do it, who else could have? Helen refused to say if anyone had visited her that day, or could have got into the house during the night.'

'It's very like this affair of her supposed suicide, isn't it?' said Mavis. 'She won't say if anyone came to see her after we'd gone out.'

'But we know someone could have got in through the kitchen window,' Reg explained. 'We don't think she did attempt suicide,' he added, for the Bradleys' benefit. 'If she had she'd have put on the gas in her room, or else put her head in the oven. It'd be crazy to turn it on in the kitchen and wait for it to seep upstairs. That's proved by the fact that it wasn't lethal.'

'It'd have been lethal to Joy,' said Mavis, shuddering. 'If we'd been at home.'

Mrs Bradley drew a long breath.

'Perhaps that was what was intended. A second child murder. That would have finished her, whatever else happened. Blackened her name if she'd died, and sent her to the gallows if she hadn't.'

'Or certified her insane,' said Mr Bradley, gruffly.

He appeared to be as shaken as his wife by these revelations and theories.

'You agree, then,' persisted Reg, 'that someone is definitely gunning for her, and may have been from the start, way back in Conington when they planned to murder that child?'

'I wouldn't go so far as that,' answered the farmer, cautiously. 'What about motive?'

'Suppose the child was Frances's. She'd married Mr Meadows. Miss Trubb says she can't keep it any longer. Their father has died. Any scandal isn't her responsibility any more. Frances can't face it. She kills the child, and lets Helen take the blame, knowing she will do so.'

'If Frances or anyone else did such a devilish thing to poor Helen,' said Mrs Bradley, 'I'll go to any lengths to help you prove it. But I'm afraid there's nothing we *can* do.'

Reg leaned forward eagerly.

'Would you really, Mrs Bradley? Go to any lengths, I mean? Because you could help. You already have.'

'How?'

'I'll tell you. Do you remember saying just now that the last time you saw Frances in Weyford before the baby's birth was April? Well, it was born in July, wasn't it? Did you see her early April, or late? Was she in a big coat or not?'

'Reg!' said Mavis. 'You are awful!'

'No,' Mrs Bradley said, smiling round at her. 'He's a father, isn't he? I see what you mean,' she went on to Reg. 'I might be able to check on it.'

'That and any other dates she was at home, between the time Helen went away in February, and that April. Who saw her and where, and for how long, and what she was wearing.'

'She was away, I do remember, when Helen went,' said Mr Bradley, who had been flogging his memory. 'I was on leave at the time, myself. She was doing this camouflage stuff, on factories in Conington, old Clements told me.'

'In an arty overall, I bet,' said Reg. 'Very convenient.'

'There were one or two other girls from the art school in the same job, I believe. But I don't remember the others being so far away. Mostly on local stuff, army camps near here. And not for long, after it was properly organized.'

'I wish we'd worked this out at the time. Don't you, Bob?' said his wife, regretfully.

'I'm not sure we didn't,' answered Mr Bradley. 'But we can't have come to any conclusion, or we'd have told Coke.'

'It could only be a negative conclusion,' Reg pointed out.

'No one would have given it any weight, then. But it would help us now, or it might do so.'

With this Mavis got up to go. The Bradleys had done much more than either she or Reg had expected. They had been most kind. It would not do to trespass on their time or their good nature any further at present. Besides, Joy was getting restless, and it was time to get her home to her bath, supper and bed.

But Reg had other ideas. When they reached the turning into the Portsmouth Road, instead of joining the steady stream of cars heading back to London after a day in the country, he waited patiently until he could cross to the other side and then headed back towards Weyford.

'For Heaven's sake!' cried Mavis. 'What are we doing this for?'

'It's a chance in a million,' said Reg. 'We know the Bradleys gave the letter with the map to Colin or Frances to post. I'm going to ask them what they did with it.'

'You're not! You can't! If either of them opened the letter and changed the map, they aren't likely to say so. We can't *accuse* them of it!'

'Not directly. But we may get them off balance. They may not have heard anything yet.'

'Of course they'll have heard. That sort of thing gets around at once. Reg, we can't let them see we suspect them! If we're right, they're *dangerous!*'

'I'd rather know who we've got to deal with, than keep on in the dark, as we are.'

'I'd rather give it all up. Leave it to the police, where it belongs.'

'A fat lot they'll do!'

They drove on in silence. When Reg turned into the drive at Downside, Mavis refused to get out of the car.

'I'd sooner stay here with Joy,' she said. 'I don't want her frightened again like the last time.'

There was no answer to this. Reg merely said, 'O.K., I'll manage,' and began to get out of the car.

'She was nice to us,' Mavis said, as he turned to shut the door. 'I shouldn't have the face to ask her what she did with the letter.'

'It's him I want to see,' said Reg. 'He may throw me out, but it's worth trying.'

Colin Meadows was at home, alone, it seemed. He did not throw Reg out. On the contrary, he gave him a cigarette, pointed to a chair and asked him why Mavis had not come in with him. Reg explained that she was looking after Joy in the car, and that in any case he would not be staying more than five minutes.

'It was just about a letter to me that Mr Bradley of Stowe Farm asked you to post, a week ago,' he said.

'Ah!' Mr Meadows leaned back in his chair. Very smoothly and clearly he told Reg the various movements of the letter. 'Frances would bear me out,' he finished, 'but she is in her room. The shock of Leslie's death has upset her. She knows his wife very well, as I have just told you.'

'Are you referring to the – accident?' Reg asked. 'I mean the one I reported to the police?'

'To Leslie Coke's death,' said Mr Meadows. 'Surely the Bradleys told you who he was?'

'No, they didn't. I don't think they knew at the time. The police sergeant told me he knew the man, but not his name. It had nothing to do with me, had it?'

Reg's expression was one of slightly indignant innocence. He hoped he was not overdoing it.

'No,' said Mr Meadows, regarding him thoughtfully. 'No, nothing whatever. About that letter. Bob Bradley rang me up after you rang him up, at lunch time today. We had not heard from Leslie's wife, then, of course. That news came later. Bob was upset about the map he had sent you in his letter. He asked me where I had posted it.'

'He asked about the map, did he? Not just about the letter?'

'We had seen the letter. He showed it to us, my wife and me. Also the map. Before putting them in the envelope and asking us to post them.'

Mr Meadows stared coldly at Reg. The latter could do nothing except mumble agreement. Bradley had indeed told him that the Meadows knew the contents of the letter.

'Is there anything else I can do for you?' asked Mr Meadows. It was a plain dismissal.

Reg got up. Mavis had been right. It had been a mistake to come here with a silly question about the map. If it wasn't just a plain insult it was a stupid move that gave away his suspicions, however vague they might be.

In an attempt to leave on a more friendly note he said, politely, Were you in the R.A.F. in the war, sir?'

'No,' Mr Meadows answered, moving to his side.

'I only asked, because I see you have a photo of Mrs Meadows in the W.A.A.F.'

They looked at the photograph, an enlarged snapshot in which Frances, young and smiling, and very pretty in her becoming uniform, stood beside a parked motor-cycle.

'She was a dispatch rider,' said Mr Meadows. 'Silly picture, really. They dressed them up differently, of course, when they were on the job. Crash helmet, and padded clothes. I took that when she was on leave.'

They went out into the drive. As reg moved round the bonnet of his car he passed the open door of the Meadows's garage. There was a car inside, and next to it a motor-bike, very generously caked with mud. He did not pause, but opened his own car door and got into the driver's seat.

Mavis wound down the window on her side as Mr Meadows stepped forward.

'I hope you didn't mind Reg calling,' she said, apologetically.

'Not a bit. I hope I was able to help him.'

'Thank you,' said Reg, leaning across with a radiant smile. 'You certainly did.'

Mr Meadows smiled pleasantly, himself, and retreated to the front steps of his house. Reg turned the car and drove away.

'Well?' Mavis asked, a few minutes later. But Reg had forgotten the letter in a new excitement.

'Did you see that bike in their garage?' he asked.

'Of course I did. What's more I got out to have a look at it near to. As there was no one in sight.'

'Good girl. Anything special?'

'It was too dark to see properly. There was a lot of mud, and a great long piece of bramble round the rear mudguard.'

Reg whistled.

'The motor-bike tracks in that lane were very close to the verge, and there were plenty of brambles there,' he said. 'What's more, Frances used one in the W.A.A.F. during the war. It isn't a thing you'd forget.'

CHAPTER 14

In Superintendent Mitchell's room at Scotland Yard a gloomy silence prevailed. It was still unbroken when the door opened to admit Inspector Frost and Sergeant Willis.

'You know Brown, don't you?' Mitchell asked.

The newcomers nodded.

'Right. I thought we might get together on this Coke murder. Your Chief Constable wants us to take a hand, as no doubt you've heard. So I thought we might sort out our ideas and pool the facts up to date. The only salient point, so far, leading to a reasonable motive, is that he was a blackmailer. Am I right?'

'Quite right,' Frost answered, 'and a very careful, very nasty one at that.'

'Which means,' went on the Superintendent, 'that he most likely got what was coming to him. There have been suspicions of his activites before, haven't there?'

'There have, indeed. A suicide in Weyford three years back.'

Inspector Brown spoke for the first time since the others arrived.

'Why should a chap in his position go in for blackmail?'

'He was a hopeless gambler all his life,' Frost answered. 'Did quite well as a commando in the war; probably enjoyed it as a very big gamble. He was clever enough to have been a success in any reasonable walk in life. He passed his exams in accountancy without any trouble after the war. But he dabbled in all manner of shady projects and a lot of them failed, so he was chronically short of money. At the time of his death I know he was getting desperate. People he had swindled, or half swindled, were getting bolder. He had sold his car, and went about on a motor-bike.'

'You think he was near to being run in for fraud? Or to going bankrupt?'

'Very likely. On the other hand we've found out he was receiving fairly large sums in recent months. Admittedly they were all mopped up by what he had to give back in private settlements of his queer transactions. He must have wanted to avoid open bankruptcy at all costs. The interesting thing is that the money began to come in again soon after Miss Trubb's release.'

'Ah!' said Brown. 'Now we're getting to it.'

The Superintendent nodded.

'Was he blackmailing her?' he asked.

'I doubt it. She had no money apart from her salary, and nothing to hide except her indentity, and that was already known to her employer. From what we know of her she was afraid of being attacked literally, physically, not of being blackmailed.'

'Besides, blackmailers don't kill the goose that lays the golden eggs.'

'On the other hand *she* might have wanted to get rid of *him*, if she was afraid he was after her life. But why should he be, or anyone else for that matter?'

Superintendent Mitchell looked at the two inspectors in turn.

'We seem to be forced back to the old story of Miss Trubb,' he said, 'and the rather remarkable work of those young people she was living with. If she was innocent of everything from the start, as they believe, then she has always been a potential danger to the real mother of the child and to the real killer, who may or may not be one and the same person. If she was innocent, she may at any time decide to speak the truth. This was less likely to be believed while she was in prison. There was also the hope that she might die before the end of her sentence. Also she could not be got at, in any case. But free, the danger revived and intensified. Don't you agree?'

'Absolutely,' said Inspector Brown. 'There's no doubt she's scared, and a fair suspicion she has good reason to be. There's

132

no doubt attempts have been made to discourage the Holmeses. If you want to tie Leslie in with Miss Trubb, I should say he was blackmailing, not her, but the person or persons who made her the victim of their own crimes. With her death the past would die out, and the reason for blackmail with it.'

'So what we want to know,' said Mitchell, 'is the real connection between Leslie and Miss Trubb.'

'You mean Leslie and Mrs Meadows, really, don't you?' said Inspector Frost. 'We've tried to establish if she has paid out any large sums, but we haven't succeeded. On the other hand she may have sold jewellery or other valuables. We haven't gone very far with it, yet. Not without a more definite lead in her direction.'

'We shall have to take it up with Conington,' said Mitchell. 'I've got the details as far as Reg Holmes went, which wasn't very far. The birth certificate could well have been a piece of deliberate deception by Frances. On the other hand there'd be the notification of the birth by the midwife to the Public Health Department. Holmes didn't think of that; probably didn't know of it. And then the Health Visitor might help us, too.'

The others nodded.

'Establish Frances had that child, and Leslie knew, and knew the father, and we can go ahead,' said Frost. 'She could be responsible for all the rest. Only I don't see a woman delivering a blow that would break a man's skull with the force his was cracked. She's got a good alibi, too, for the whole of Sunday. So has her husband.'

'But the motor-bike?'

'If you're going by a bit of mud and bramble, you'll find both in almost any coppice in Surrey,' said Sergeant Willis. 'Certainly on the golf-course, where Mr Meadows was playing that morning. I mean at the sides of it, you understand. He had the bike with him, too.'

'Where is the golf-course?'

'Between Weyford and Woking. I don't deny it lies not more than a couple of miles from the place where Coke was found. Are you trying to throw suspicion on Meadows, too?'

'I just wondered.'

'Then you've forgotten one thing.'

'Have I?'

'If Frances was paying blackmail, it was to hide her guilty secret from her husband, wasn't it? So he wouldn't know any more than the general public about Miss Trubb's past, or that of Frances, either.'

The Superintendent nodded. These chaps were keen. It was a pleasure to work with them.

'One thing more,' he said. 'Assuming we're right so far, how did Leslie find out where Miss Trubb was when she left Holloway?'

'A man called Thorne,' said Inspector Brown. 'Mr Reeve put me on to him. He's supposed to be the other man in Frances's past. I had a word with him after I got his name and address. He agreed that he'd recognized Helen, and said he found her very changed, not to say peculiar. According to Thorne she told him she wanted to have nothing to do with her past, friends, relations or anything. She asked him not to tell her sister where she was. He promised that, and he says he kept his promise.'

'There was no mention of Coke at that time?'

'None.'

'And now?'

Inspector Brown shook his head.

'I haven't been able to contact him,' he said. 'Following this blackmail line, I went to his place again to question him about Leslie. But he was out. In fact he has not been back to his lodgings since the evening of the day Coke was murdered.'

Warrington-Reeve astonished Reg and Mavis by appearing on their doorstep the following Saturday afternoon. They had only just finished lunch, and Mavis was washing up, while Reg played with his small daughter. He left her to go to the front door.

'I want you to come up to Conington with me,' the barrister announced. 'Is that possible?'

'When?'

'Now.'

Reg took the unexpected visitor into the sitting-room. Joy, overcome by shyness, howled her loudest. Mavis went to the rescue, hands still wet from the sink. Mr Warrington-Reeve, not in the least put out by the confusion he had caused, settled himself comfortably in a chair near the fire and lit one of his own cigarettes.

The turmoil subsided. Mavis, pulling herself together, made coffee. Twenty minutes later Reg found himself speeding towards Conington behind the long black bonnet of Warrington-Reeve's Jaguar.

'It was lucky Carol could have Mavis and Joy at such short notice,' Reg said, as the car left the North Circular, and the needle moved up to seventy. 'You're a very fast worker, sir, aren't you?'

'It's a question of knowing what you want,' said the barrister. 'Choose a simple and direct objective, and the detail has a way of settling itself.'

'Is that what we're after? A simple and direct objective?'

'Yes. We have to find out who could have got into your Mrs Ogden's former house the night Miss Trubb was alone in it, and how he or she did so.'

'Have we a definite choice of people, now? It's what Mavis and I have thought all along.'

'Quite. There's Frances, for a start. She was there a few days before the fatal night. She might have gone again. Her alibi at the trial was never questioned. There's Colin. He had been in an Army convalescent home in the neighbourhood though he had left it to go home, with Frances, the day she visited her sister. And Leslie Coke, the commando, was in England on leave.'

The word convalescent stung Reg's memory.

'The boys in blue,' he exclaimed. 'That's what Mrs Ogden called them. The convalescents from the hospital. All day long, going into the public gardens. That was when I asked her if any suspicious characters had been near her house.'

'And of course wounded soldiers couldn't be suspicious characters,' said Warrington-Reeve, softly. He pressed his foot down. They took the next stretch of road at eighty-five.

Mrs Ogden was delighted to see Reg again, and to be introduced to his distinguished friend. She listened to a guarded

and discreet account of their purpose in coming all that way
to see her.

'So much better than writing,' said the barrister, 'and so
much pleasanter.'

Mrs Ogden smiled and blushed.

'I understand it happened in a house in another part of the
town,' he went on. 'Some distance from here, I suppose?'

'Well, yes. You see, I wanted to avoid the publicity. And
in any case the neighbourhood had altered a lot − for the
worse, if you see what I mean.'

'Quite.'

There was a moment's silence and then the barrister said,
'Tell me, Mrs Ogden, did you have the same system with
regard to keys, as you have here?'

'Keys?'

'Yes. I notice you don't have a board in your office for
room keys, as one usually finds in hotels.'

'You *have* got a sharp eye, haven't you?'

'I'm sorry.'

'Don't mention it,' said Mrs Ogden, relenting. 'No, they
keep their own keys. It's safer, really, as I'm in and out all
the time. And the staff so changeable.'

'I understand. But above the table in the hall there is a key
hanging on a hook. That is a front door key, is it not?'

Mrs Ogden began to look flustered. 'Well, yes. They don't
have keys to the front door. It's not kept locked in the
daytime. But I shut everything up at night at eleven. If any
of them is going to be out late, they take that key to let
themselves in by.'

'What happens when there is more than one out late?'

'They tell me if the key has gone already, and I give them
mine. Or they can knock, though I don't encourage it. We
mostly keep early hours, you see. My guests are all in business. They don't gad about much of an evening, especially
now there's the "telley".'

'I see.' The barrister smiled at her again. Mrs Ogden smiled
back. She did not see much point in his questions, but he was
a very agreeable gentleman.

This conversation took place on Saturday evening. Before
they went back to the hotel where Warrington-Reeve had

taken rooms for them both, he drove to Mrs Ogden's old address, parking the car in a side road.

The public gardens were closed, but they were evidently still in use, for the board above the gate, announcing the hours of opening, was freshly painted, as were the iron gate itself and the railings.

'That must be the old guest house,' said the barrister, pointing across the road to a shabby-looking house in a row of equally dreary dwellings. 'Very easy to keep an eye on it, you see, from just inside, or just outside, these gardens. Easy to watch people going out and coming in and choose your time accordingly.'

'At around four in the morning?' said Reg, with raised eyebrows.

'Ah, no! That is stage three. Don't go so fast. I am describing stage one. Stage two is where the ill-intentioned person, having watched Miss Trubb go off to work, goes up to the house, and asks for a room, or for anything else that leaves him alone in the hall for a few seconds.'

'Meaning Leslie, in his commando uniform? Gosh!' Reg exclaimed. 'Mrs Ogden said she had all sorts asking for rooms, officers even.'

'I was thinking of "a boy in blue",' said Warrington-Reeve.

'*Not* Colin Meadows?'

'Why not? He could well have been around.'

'And seen his wife go in to talk to her sister? No, she didn't have to keep that from him. But he could have had his doubts, I suppose? Good God, do you think he knew all the time the child was his wife's?'

'I wouldn't be at all surprised.'

'And knew she was the murderess? Guessed it was her child and that she must have killed it? But then Frances was paying blackmail, wasn't she? He'd guess that, too. And he never told her! The absolute stinker!'

Warrington-Reeve nodded.

'I'd go further. I'd suggest it wasn't a suspicion, but that either Raymond Thorne or Leslie *told* him, previously. I'd suggest Colin had a very good motive for getting rid of Leslie. Now, let's go over the road and take a look at the rear of the house.'

He moved away, Reg following and protesting.

'Can we do that?'

'Reg, you are altogether too law-abiding. Don't you see there isn't even a gate to the back yard? Gone for firewood, I suspect, years ago. And don't you see that long strip of bell-pushes beside the front door? If anyone sees us they will merely imagine we are visiting the inmates of one of the other rooms.'

No one looked out at them from the curtained lighted windows above, as they inspected the decayed little yard at the back of the house; no one came out of the back door as they moved near and stared through uncurtained windows into two dark empty rooms on the ground floor.

'Ghastly place!' said Reg. 'But easy enough to burgle. You could get in through that small window there, any time, if you had a knife with you to lift the catch. Easy as pie.'

'I'm sure you're right. Or by the simple subterfuge I mentioned of calling to find out if Mrs Ogden had a room, learning all about the geography of the place from the inside, including, I expect, an explanation of that rather casual key system of hers.'

'He couldn't just pinch it from under her nose?'

'No. But he could watch Mrs Ogden go out and then call and ask the maid – she must have had at least a daily even in the war – for a glass of water, or something of that sort.'

Reg stared, horrified.

'If he was a convalescent! Someone to be pitied!'

'And take the key while he was alone in the hall. And put it back later.'

'When he'd smothered that poor kid. Mrs Ogden would never suspect that was how it had gone, when it turned up she'd just think one of her guests had forgotten to put it back until he found it in his pocket, or something.'

'Don't let us go too fast,' said Warrington-Reeve. 'Let us go back to Mrs Ogden, and ask her if she ever missed the front door key, and let us show her some photographs.'

'What photos?' gasped Reg. The pace of the day's work was leaving him behind.

'Only some I collected at the time of the trial,' said Warrington-Reeve. 'Of all the characters concerned. And a

138

few I've been able to pick up since. From a member of that commando unit, for example, and from one of the R.A.M.C. doctors who was working at the convalescent hospital at the time.'

'What we really want is the daily. The one you said must have opened the door to him.'

'Reg, Reg!' reproved Warrington-Reeve. 'You really mustn't be so impressionable! I want you as a witness, not as a member of the jury.'

The routine work of the police continued. At Weyford the inquest on Leslie Coke was adjourned. Dragging operations in the river had brought up a strange assortment of blunt instruments, from pieces of old bedsteads to broken plough-shares. But nothing that was likely to have been used on Leslie. Examinations of his business books and records had disclosed many strange deviations from legitimate practice, and many transactions that could not be checked at all accurately. On the whole his career had taken a downward direction. His wife could give no help except to confirm this fact, and her bewilderment at it. She was a silly woman, cherishing wholly superficial values, but not dishonest. Clearly she had never suspected her husband of anything more than persistent ill luck.

The Meadows' alibis were gone into more thoroughly. While both were plausible, it was now found that neither was completely cast-iron. Frances had gone to church, taking the car, but had arrived home only just in time for lunch. She had made a detour to look at the country, she said, because it was such a lovely morning. Curiously enough, her husband had done precisely the same thing, after leaving the club house. It left very little time for either of them to arrange the events at the bridge, and on the whole Inspector Frost was rendered less suspicious than if the alibis had been perfect. The only satisfactory piece of evidence came from a farm hand, who volunteered the information that he had been on his way to the Hen and Chicken just before one and had seen the Road Closed notice propped against the hedge at the entrance to the lane, with the trestle underneath it. So he had put it back in its proper place. Boys, he had thought at the time, and decided to say nothing about it. He had gone home before the police arrived, so he did not hear of the excitement at the pub until the evening, when he paid his second visit of the day there. It took him a day or two after that to decide to state what he had done.

Inspector Brown made several attempts to find the missing artist, but with no success. He had been out all day, his landlady said, but had come in about five; with very muddy shoes and mud up his trousers, she added, indignantly. She had taken him up a pot of tea to his studio, and then gone out to her sister's, to watch the television. When she came back she went straight to bed. Mr Thorne was not there in the morning, his bed had not been slept in, but his things were all in his room. She had not seen him since.

No one had seen him. None of his known associates had any clue to his whereabouts. There was really nothing to connect him with Leslie Coke, except that distant rivalry for the young Frances Clement's affections. It was all a bit absurd, the Inspector thought. Artists are known to be eccentric.

The mental hospital could not help him. Dr Bauer, Miss Trubb's doctor, told him that though she was not on parole now, she seemed to be able to evade the porters from time to time, and go out by herself. She had been out until quite late, or at least had been absent from her villa until quite late, on the Sunday in question. They were not prepared to have her certified. She was a voluntary patient, and could leave when she liked. The question of parole did not really apply to her, but most of the patients, even the voluntary ones, responded to the mild discipline involved. She was definitely not dangerous to other people.

'He says that, in spite of her record,' grumbled Inspector Frost to Sergeant Willis. 'Always on the side of the criminal, these psychos.'

In Conington Superintendent Mitchell made more progress. With the patience and resource of normal police methods, the Public Health Department was induced to comb its records. Two important pieces of information emerged. The midwife who had notified the birth had put down the mother's surname as Clements, not Trubb. Following this up, Mitchell discovered that one of the Health Visitors had been a close friend of this midwife at the time, and had renewed the friendship later, Very fortunately she was still working in the district.

'It was a good bit later we started corresponding again,' she explained. 'Actually not till some time after the trial. I remember they asked me at the time if I knew where she was. Miss Trubb's lawyers, that would be. But I didn't know. She didn't write till after the end of the war. She married in Canada, as I expect you know. But I've heard from her regularly ever since. She wants me to go out there when I retire next summer.'

'Then you can give us her address?'

'Oh, yes.'

Mitchell explained why they wanted it, and went on to say that he was surprised she had not been called by the defence at the trial.

'Because I never had anything to do with the case, personally. It must have been this muddle with the names. The Health Visitor would be given the name on the notification card, Clements in this case, and go round to see the mother. It wasn't me. Did the baby attend the clinic?'

More records were consulted. Baby Clements was never brought to any clinic. Nor was Baby Trubb. Mitchell understood why the Health Visitor had not appeared at the trial. Miss Trubb really seemed to have done everything she could to convict herself.

The news from Canada came promptly and was perfectly definite. The midwife remembered the case, because it had seemed to her a bit of a mystery. The two girls evidently belonged to quite an educated and respectable family. She had been very much impressed by the devotion of the elder sister. The unmarried mother's name was Frances Clements, but she and her sister Helen had passed themselves off under the queer name of Trubb.

CHAPTER 15

The news from Canada filled both Reg and Mavis with more awe than pleasure. Looking back at the events of the last two and a half months they realized what they had done. It would have been so easy, and so much more expected of them, to write of Miss Trubb as a terrible mistake, a narrow shave, anyway, something they would avoid in future. Instead, they had gone to her support with altogether unasked and unwanted enthusiasm. They had set about tearing up her history, knocking holes in the wall she had set round herself, digging out the evil that had gone to earth with her imprisonment. It seemed a lot to have done, just by being inquisitive and sticking to the idea they had formed of their lodger.

'What's going to happen now?' asked Mavis.

'You'll get your Mum back here, for a start,' said Reg. 'Someone's on the run, and the cops are not far behind, and we won't take any chances.'

'We're out of it now, aren't we?'

'I'm not sure. Whoever it is can't be sure, either.'

So Mrs Ford came back to Twenty-six Sandfields Avenue and Mavis was glad to have her, danger or no danger. Joy was beginning to crawl and took a lot of watching all the time she was awake, to see she didn't get into mischief or hurt herself.

Mrs Ford listened to all the latest developments with admirable calm.

'I wonder the police let you know the results of their work,' she said at the end.

'They didn't. At least this Scotland Yard chap, Mitchell,

did tell Mr Warrington-Reeve he'd traced the midwife concerned, so naturally he cabled her and got the answer he wanted. That Frances Meadows was the real mother of the child.'

Mrs Ford thought this over for some time without speaking. 'I can understand Frances deceiving her sister and passing the child off on her if she was getting herself engaged to Mr Meadows,' she said, at last. 'But she must have thought it out before, long before.'

'She's supposed to have been flighty and all that,' said Mavis. 'It doesn't go with such a cold-blooded lying plot. The birth certificate, too. She had a nerve. And she must have thought that one up, too, long before the baby was born.'

'Long before anyone knew the midwife wouldn't be there to give her the lie back,' said Reg. 'Nerve isn't the word for it. It was plain crazy.'

'She must have been darned sure of Helen,' said Mavis sadly. 'Poor Miss Trubb.'

'She spoiled her, didn't she?' said Mrs Ford. 'The more you give that sort, the more they'll take.'

Mavis nodded.

'Will anyone have told her?'

'Who? Mrs Meadows?'

'Oh, no. Mrs Trubb.'

Reg shook his head.

'Shouldn't think so. What'd be the point?'

'It might relieve her mind.'

'I don't see how.'

'To know that the secret's out at last, for what it's worth now.'

'What is it worth?' asked Mrs Ford, 'now that Mr Coke is dead? He was the blackmailer, wasn't he? And the father of the baby, perhaps?'

They were checked by this, but Mavis still felt an urge to go to the hospital, in spite of Reg's doubts.

'It can't do any harm,' she told her mother the next morning. 'Even if it doesn't do any good.'

'All right. You go. I'll see to Joy,' said Mrs Ford, placidly.

Mavis was told that Miss Trubb had been in bed for a few

days, with a relapse, but was now better. As she had never, in Mavis's opinion, been ill, she asked what the relapse was from. The nurse gave her a queer look.

'Her mental condition, of course,' she said. This was so vague, and at the same time so final, that Mavis decided not to ask any more questions.

'Can I see her?' she asked.

'I expect so.'

After a short wait, Miss Trubb arrived in charge of another nurse, who merely brought her to the door of the visitors' room, saw her go in, and shut the door after her.

Miss Trubb looked just the same as usual, Mavis thought, except for her eyes. In the old days when she was with them at Sandfields Avenue, she had always looked you straight in the face. Now her glance flickered towards Mavis and away and back again, until finally she moved to the window and stood there with her back to the room, quite silent and still.

'Miss Trubb,' said Mavis, disturbed by this behaviour, 'I – I hope you don't mind my coming.'

'Of course not.' The voice was quiet without expression.

'We worry about you, you know.'

'I am perfectly well.'

'They said you'd – had a relapse. Been in bed, I mean.'

'I had a slight feverish cold. It is better now.'

Mavis began to doubt the wisdom of her visit. Ought she to give her disturbing news to Miss Trubb in her present condition? Would it make her worse still?'

While she sat, tongue-tied, wondering what to do, Miss Trubb left the window and, coming nearer, sat down. She smiled gently. She was looking at Mavis now with all her old sympathy and understanding.

'You didn't come here on account of my health,' she said. 'Or not for that only. What have you to tell me?'

Mavis did not hesitate.

'We know that baby was not yours,' she said. 'You said it wasn't, and that was the truth. It was your sister's. They have found the midwife in Canada.'

Miss Trubb's face grew white and hard. She closed her eyes. Her breathing was loud in the silent room.

'I had to tell you!' Mavis cried, jumping up and putting an

144

arm across the bowed shoulders. 'You ought to know they've found out.'

'Who have found out?' whispered Miss Trubb.

'The police did it. They told Mr Reeve. He had a cable back in answer to one he sent. He told us.'

'Have they – ' Miss Trubb spoke with difficulty. 'Frances! What about Frances?'

This aspect of the news had not occurred to Reg or Mavis.

'I don't know,' she said. 'I expect they'll ask her now if Leslie Coke was blackmailing her on account of it. They were practically sure of that already. He was, wasn't he?'

'Yes,' said Miss Trubb.

'You know he's dead? Murdered?'

'Yes,' said Miss Trubb again.

'Have the police been here?'

'No. At least, not to see me. No.'

They sat looking at one another. Then Miss Trubb reached for Mavis's hand and held it in hers as she went on speaking.

'I promised my mother I would always look after Frances. When she told me that February that she was expecting a baby in the late July or early August, I didn't know how I could keep my promise. My father was strict and old-fashioned. He would have disowned her. Leslie refused to marry her.'

'Why didn't she get rid of it?'

Miss Trubb looked very shocked.

'That's a dreadful idea! I knew it was often done, but I was terrified she'd try it, and die, or maim herself for life. No proper doctor would help her, would he?'

Mavis did not answer this. Instead she said, 'You knew Leslie was the father?'

'Oh yes. She told me. I tried to persuade him, but it was no use. So we both went to Conington. You know what happened there.'

'Yes. She repaid you nicely, didn't she?'

Miss Trubb sighed.

'I think he put her up to it. Frances is weak, and she was frightened and helpless. I don't think she was capable of such a plan. He must have known us both very well. He was a wicked man.'

'She was a wicked girl!' cried Mavis, indignantly. 'Taking your own boy away from you as well.'

A look of pain crossed Miss Trubb's white face.

'Colin can never have loved me,' she said, quietly. 'It took me a long time to believe that, but I believe it now. Frances was very pretty as a girl. I'd expected him to trust me and wait for an explanation. When he thought the worst of me, I was horrified and disgusted. It was worse still when he married her. But it made it impossible for me to expose her. You see, I still loved him, so how could I ruin his happiness?'

Mavis's eyes filled with tears. Miss Trubb patted her hand gently.

'I liked having little Tom,' she said. 'I knew I should never love again, or marry, or have children of my own. I suppose I was old-fashioned, like my father.'

Mavis burst out, passionately, 'You took the blame for his death, knowing your sister did it?'

Miss Trubb bowed her head.

'She came to see me a few days before he – died,' she said. 'She told me she was desperate. Leslie had been getting money from her, threatening to tell Colin. He had blackmailed her from the time she had the child. She paid him then to prevent him telling Father, because he'd have cut her off as he did me. She could pay him then, because she was in the W.A.A.F. But after she married Colin it was more difficult. She came to me, because Father was dead, and she would inherit, but it would take time to get probate and settle everything, and Leslie wouldn't wait, she said. I told her the best thing would be to tell Colin, and have done with it. Or else go to the police. I even said I might tell Colin myself to save her from the blackmail. I dinned it into her that Leslie knew she was now a wealthy woman and his threats meant nothing. He'd wait for his money all right. Blackmailers always did. She was very angry with me and went away. Tom died three days later.'

'She murdered her own child,' said Mavis.

Miss Trubb rocked backwards and forwards in her chair. The old agony was upon her again, even now, after all the years of expiation, of doubt, of grief.

'It was my fault. I drove her to it. So it was right to take the blame. They thought they could prove me guilty. Even if I had spoken, they would not have been able to prove anything against her. But her life would have been ruined, and Colin's life, and their children's. I couldn't speak, could I?'

'Nothing was your fault,' said Mavis, soothingly. 'But I came to prepare you, because they are going to find out who killed Leslie Coke and if that was Frances, too – '

'No,' said Miss Trubb very firmly. 'That was not Frances.'

'How do you know?'

Miss Trubb's face suddenly collapsed into a vague stupidity. Mavis was shocked and frightened.

'How do you know?' she asked again, shrilly insistent.

'Tell them to ask Raymond Thorne,' said Miss Trubb. 'I saw him on the Sunday night you had your experience at Tilbey. Tell them to ask him.' She stared past Mavis, sullen and withdrawn.

'But – but what do you know about our experience? Who told you?'

'It was in the papers,' said Miss Trubb. 'I read the papers.'

'Then you must know that Mr Thorne is missing.'

'Missing?'

'You might not realize. They didn't give his name. They only said a man who could help in the inquiries.'

'*Raymond* missing?' Miss Trubb returned to her normal manner, but her eyes were troubled. 'Oh dear! Oh dear, what have I been saying, I wonder?'

It was a schoolboy, on his way home across Wimbledon Common with some friends, who found Raymond Thorne, three days after Mavis had seen Miss Trubb.

They were throwing a ball to each other when the smallest of them missed a catch and the ball, skimming off the tips of his fingers, disappeared into a clump of bushes, some distance from the footpath. He ran to find it and a few minutes later ran back, faster than before and yelling with a fright.

Raymond Thorne's body was not a pleasant sight. Half covered with fallen leaves and in an advanced state of decay, the boy had not seen it until he tripped over a muddy leather shoe. The ankle bones, unsupported by flesh, had cracked apart, and there was a shoe, with the remains of a foot in it, and beyond, just where the ball lay, the remains of a face.

The biggest of the older boys went into the bushes and came out yellow-faced and sickly. The younger boy cried and shook. But they did not lose their heads. Though none of them agreed to guard the place in the gathering dusk, they marked it carefully, and went off in a group to the police station, where their looks and manner confirmed their report. The body was recovered and taken to the mortuary.

The cause of death was not easily established. The man must have been lying there for at least a fortnight, the pathologist said. It had been a wet season, and warm for November. Thorne had been stout. The tissues had decayed readily.

'You can't give us the day he died?' Inspector Brown asked.

'Not the exact day. About a fortnight.'

'Was he alive last Sunday week?'

'The point is,' said Superintendent Mitchell, who had just arrived at the mortuary, 'could he have killed Leslie Coke?'

'He might. I simply can't say.'

'Could Coke have killed him?'

The pathologist shook his head.

'It's no good. I can say he was probably alive that Sunday. I can now say he did not die of any natural disease, though he was far from healthy. He may have been strangled. What's left of the lungs and trachea is not conclusive of that, and the hyoid bones are intact. But they might well escape, with a covering of fat such as he had to cushion them from pressure. It might have been suicide by drugs. You'll have to wait for the analysis.'

Inspector Brown did not wait for long. The next day Roy Holmes saw the news of Thorne's death, and took Mavis's information to the police station. The inspector at once told Mitchell, who went to the hospital and asked for Dr Bauer.

'I hope she'll co-operate at last,' he said, when he had put the position to the psychiatrist. 'At least we know from her own statement to Mrs Holmes she saw Thorne that Sunday evening, *after* the death of Leslie Coke.'

'I'm sorry,' said Dr Bauer, and for once his controlled impassive face showed real agitation. 'She was a voluntary patient, you know. She left us yesterday.'

'Why didn't you report that?' barked the Superintendent.

'I have not so far had an opportunity. You have been explaining the situation.'

'Yesterday, sir. Yesterday. Why didn't you report to us as soon as she left?'

'You have never asked me to report to you. I would not in any case, have consented to that. The police must do their own work. This is not a criminal lunatic asylum, whatever Miss Trubb's record may be. My job is to treat patients, not spy on them.'

The mutual lack of confidence was complete. Superintendent Mitchell swallowed the criticism that rose to his lips.

'Where's she gone?' he demanded, gruffly. 'What address?'

'She left no fresh address. She said inquiries would find her at the old one.'

'Which was?'

'Twenty-six Sandfields Avenue,' said Dr Bauer, reading from Miss Trubb's case sheet.

Mitchell exclaimed angrily.

'That's where the Holmeses live. She won't have gone *there*.'

'It is possible,' Dr Bauer smiled faintly. 'There is not very much the matter with Miss Trubb, medically speaking, and now that these two men are dead – '

But Superintendent Mitchell was already half-way to the door, so the psychiatrist did not bother to finish his sentence.

CHAPTER 16

'I have a surprise for you,' said Warrington-Reeve.

Reg waited. He was learning fast. You had to give people their head and then you might get good value for your patience. As now.

'Miss Trubb is back at work in Philpot's office,' the barrister announced.

'Well, I'm blowed!' This was a first-class surprise indeed. 'How did you know?'

'Philpot rang me up this morning. Not only is she back at work, but Mrs Philpot has given her a room in their house for the time being.'

'But – but the Yard?' stammered Reg. 'I understood she'd disappeared on account of having told Mavis she'd seen Thorne the night Leslie was killed, and maybe she'd done in both of them.'

'That theory seems to have been shelved for the moment,' said Warrington-Reeve, 'unless Mitchell is keeping something very much up his sleeve. I don't expect him to tell me what he's doing, or what he's found. The Coke murder and Thorne's death are no business of mine. The only information he's given me relates to past history, I mean, of course, the parentage of the child, Tom.'

Reg nodded.

'Does that actually alter anything connected with the murder? You've always said it didn't.'

'Only in so far as it provides a motive, at last, for Frances wishing to get rid of the child, to stop the blackmail. The only snag is she was definitely not in Conington the night the child died. She was in her own home. There are witnesses of that. It was never questioned, as I told you before. Colin is another story.'

'Mrs Ogden didn't recognize his photo, did she?'

Unfortunately, no. So we have still no support for our fascinating theory of the "boy in blue".'

'On the other hand she recognized Leslie, didn't she? At least, she said she'd seen that face before.'

'No. I've another disappointment for you, there. I made a mistake over that early photo. It happened to be one of Stephen Coke, not Leslie. There is a strong family likeness. I'm talking of the pre-war snapshot of the home putting green.'

'Not the commando one?'

But Warrington-Reeve was not listening.

'Golf!' he exclaimed. 'The Cokes played golf, too!'

Reg was mystified.

'What's that got to do with Mrs Ogden?' he asked. 'Anyway, why did she recognize Stephen?'

'Oh, my dear chap! Think. She saw him several times. At the trial. Before that in the magistrate's court. Right from the beginning, in fact.'

'But you asked her if the man in the photo had been to her house in Conington.'

'Well, so he must have. From the beginning.'

'To see Helen? Wouldn't she be in gaol?'

'He was the family lawyer,' said Warrington-Reeve, thoughtfully. 'I wonder if he went to see her after her father's death. It's very likely, if he managed to get her address from Frances. Yes, it's very likely,' he repeated, 'to break the news of her disinheritance gently. I'll make a point of asking him.'

At Scotland Yard Mitchell studied the pathologist's report of the remains of Raymond Thorne.

'Death due to poisoning,' he reflected. 'A lethal dose of barbiturate. No evidence as yet as to how it could have been administered, or obtained, I suppose? Though suicide seems a bit unlikely. Mid-November, under bushes on the Common.'

'Quite.' Inspector Brown followed up with his own report. 'Thorne did not consult any of our local doctors at any time.

No chemist in our district made up a prescription for him for drugs of any sort. In that connection Dr Evenett, Miss Trubb's doctor, only gave her a mild tablet containing aspirin, codeine, and a bromide derivative, so he says. That means she hadn't got any of the right stuff hidden away. Dr Bauer at the hospital says the patients are handed their doses, singly, by the nurses, who watch them take them, as prescribed. No storing up bulk doses in that hospital. Or keeping any they take in, either.'

'Which seems to let out Trubb as far as Thorne is concerned, though she did see him the evening he disappeared. What about Mrs Meadows?'

It was Inspector Frost's turn.

'She'd have had time to get up to London after I'd seen her that Sunday. They have no staff on Sunday, after midday. She had plenty of time. And she takes barbiturate regularly for insomnia. But it's a very mild kind. You'd need a lot of tablets to make up a fatal dose. I don't see how she'd get Thorne to swallow it, in any circumstances.'

'He drank a lot. If he was pretty well sozzled, he wouldn't notice what he was being given, and the mixture would add to the lethal effect.'

'Possibly. What about motive?'

'Thorne must have tipped off Coke when he located Miss Trubb. Otherwise I can't see how Leslie found out where she was. Probably Thorne sold his information. He wasn't doing much painting, and his funds were low. If Frances killed Coke, Thorne became doubly dangerous, and had to be removed as well.'

'O.K. Then did she kill Coke, and if so, how?'

They were all silent. Then Mitchell said, 'Nothing new at the Weyford end?'

'No,' said Inspector Frost. 'She had the car that morning Coke died. There were no signs of it anywhere near the lane. Colin Meadows had the motor-bike. No signs of it anywhere around there, either. The evidence young Holmes gave of its condition is quite inconclusive. All the lanes near the Golf Club are narrow and muddy, and have brambles trailing in the hedges.'

'But neither of the Meadows pair has a complete alibi?'

'That's right.'

'And Colin was out when you saw Mrs Meadows?'

'Yes.'

'But in later?'

'Not so late he couldn't have got up to London by, say, ten that evening.'

'Still no sign of a weapon?' asked Mitchell, changing the subject, which had grown unprofitable.

'No. We've been over the ground several times, and had the river dragged again. It may be there still, in the undergrowth or in the water. That would be the obvious place to chuck the thing.'

'Unless they had the sense to expect a search and decided to take it home.'

'There was a lot of blood,' said Frost.

'That would wash off in the river.'

'We thought of it, when we were looking for footprints on the bank. We didn't find any place near enough for a person to stoop down and wash anything – such as a cosh. Nor their clothes and shoes, which would be splashed with blood, almost certainly. We tried particularly hard for traces of blood on the ground, and footprints near the site of the body, but there weren't any, except the prints of Reg and Mavis Holmes. As for washing, the water was well up and running fast, but the bank is sloping, except just at the site of the bridge, where the bank is a good deal higher. Out of reach, you see, in both cases.'

'Did you say there were no footprints?'

'No. I said no prints with blood attached. There were plenty of prints on the bank. Besides the Holmeses', there were kids', and others, mostly in gum boots. That wouldn't exclude Mrs Meadows or her husband. They both have them. And she has a pair of boots she used to wear on her motorbike in the W.A.A.F. Still wears them for riding it.'

'Did you look at their boots? Were they wet or dry?'

'Damp and muddy, the lot. And both of them said they do a bit of gardening every day just now, clearing up.'

'So we can't exclude Mrs Meadows or her husband.'

'Or Miss Trubb.'

'Oh, don't know,' said Mitchell. 'I wouldn't worry about

her at present. She seems to be feeling pretty confident, to have left the hospital and gone back to work quite openly. She sent me her new address the day after I wrote to her, care of Reg Holmes, saying she must report, or take the consequences. I think we'll leave her alone for the time being.'

'What do we do then? Wait for something to turn up?' asked Inspector Brown. 'Adjourn the inquest on Thorne indefinitely?'

'I'll see the coroner,' Mitchell answered. 'No, we don't just wait. First of all we go on working at the recent payments to Leslie. We can't fix them on the Meadows couple either of them. But they must be traced. I suggest we get Stephen Coke's help in that. He's trying to sort out his cousin's affairs. It might lead us somewhere. And then I think I know where we shall find the weapon that killed Leslie. With luck we might be able to prove it was used. Which would lead us straight to the individual we want. I thought we might follow that up now.'

This conversation took place at Scotland Yard early on Friday morning. At Mr Philpot's home near Esher Miss Trubb, at breakfast the next day, announced her intention of visiting her sister in Weyford.

The Philpots knew nothing about the most recent developments in the case. Nor did Miss Trubb know anything of her employer's activities on her behalf. She had asked to go back to her job, merely explaining that she felt well enough to do so. Mr Philpot had agreed to take her, and after speaking to his wife on the phone, had suggested giving her a room in his house. Neither of them found anything strange in this arrangement, though the rest of the office staff was affronted and perplexed. However, they had liked Miss Trubb until they were confused about her by the newspaper reports, and as she seemed now to be exactly the same as before, by the end of the week she had slipped back into place, completely, and the slight friction came to an end.

It was the same at Mr Philpot's house. His wife had been surprised, a little alarmed, but willing to be charitable. By Saturday morning she was actively kind.

'You can get a Green Line bus,' she said, leaving her breakfast to find the time-table. 'I expect you'd like to ring her up and tell her when to expect you.'

Miss Trubb thanked Mrs Philpot for the time-table, but she did not use the telephone. She merely checked the time of the Saturday bus.

She arrived at Weyford about one o'clock and had lunch at a small new tea shop on the outskirts of the town, near the bus station. She got to Downside a little after two, having walked there all the way, and as she went up the drive she noticed, with satisfaction, that the car was out. Colin must have left for the Golf Club. He always had a round on Saturday afternoon, she remembered, as far back as she had known him. Her timing was just right.

Mrs Meadows was sitting in her drawing-room with her feet up, reading the local weekly paper, when Helen walked quietly into the room. She was so astonished and so frightened that she could not move, but simply lay there staring, her mouth fallen open, the colour draining from her face.

Miss Trubb went up to her very quietly, took the newspaper from her lap, where it had fallen, laid it aside, and stood looking down at her sister.

'Well, Frances,' she said. 'It's all over now, so we can't pretend any longer.'

'I don't know what you mean,' whispered Mrs Meadows.

Miss Trubb made an impatient gesture, and the younger woman shrank down on the sofa, putting up a hand to guard her face.

'Oh, yes you do,' said Miss Trubb.

She turned, found a chair, brought it close to where the other lay, and sat down.

'They know you were Tom's mother,' she said. 'They found Nurse Walters in Canada, though that isn't her name now, because she married. They've guessed Leslie was the father.'

Mrs Meadows moaned faintly. The sound exasperated her sister.

'You should have done what I told you in the first place,' she said, fiercely. 'Wasn't it enough that I took all the shame and the responsibility for Tom? Wasn't it enough that I blackened my name with Father, and cut myself off from all my friends? Wasn't it enough that I did all this for you, and never exposed your dreadful lies and tricks and cheating over the jobs and the birth certificate? What did it matter if Colin knew? You were married, weren't you? No one else need have known. No one else would have believed any story Leslie might have tried to circulate. But he wouldn't have done a thing. You knew him. You knew it was all bluff.'

'I didn't. I didn't. He began it before Colin asked me to marry him. You know he did.'

'You could have stopped it later. I told you what you ought to do.'

'Oh, yes, you always knew best,' cried Frances, dragging herself up into a sitting position. 'You made me sick, with your good advice. Always in the right, always down on me. That's why I acted as I did, all along. To get a bit of my own back. Which I did.'

Miss Trubb said, steadily, 'And was that why you killed your son?'

Frances gasped.

'*I* killed him? Have you taken leave of your senses? How dare you! How *dare* you!'

Her voice was hoarse with disgust and fear.

'You *know* I didn't! You *must* know! You *know* you did it yourself!'

'Even now,' said Miss Trubb in despair. 'Even now you can't confess your crime. Even now, when the police are closing in on you.'

'But it wasn't me!' screamed Frances, springing up from the sofa. 'It wasn't! It wasn't! I can prove it! I *did* prove it! I was here at home in Weyford. You heard the evidence. You're the one that ought to confess.'

'All these years,' said her sister, her face crumbling into tears, 'all these years you've thought me guilty! And a liar. May God forgive you!'

'What else could I think? What did you think of me?'

Miss Trubb covered her face with her hands, and rocked herself to and fro. Her sister suddenly knelt beside her.

'Helen! Helen, I'm sorry! I know it was wicked, what I did and said at the trial. I wasn't ungrateful before. I did wrong, but I was sorry. Only I thought you did kill him, and that cancelled out all you'd done. I felt then, I owed you nothing. You were as bad as me. No, worse! Far worse! That's why I acted as I did at the trial.'

Miss Trubb got out her handkerchief and dried her eyes. She put an arm round her sister, drawing her close.

'Poor Frances. We were both mad, I think. So it was never you. I must believe it, I suppose?'

'Yes, yes. You *must* believe it!'

'You didn't kill Tom, and you didn't deliberately let me be found guilty.'

'I was afraid I'd driven you to it, but I believed you guilty.' Miss Trubb sighed heavily.

'The wickedness,' she said, 'is more than I can bear.'

Frances drew away from her, and getting up from her knees, sat down again on the sofa. She did believe at last that Helen spoke the truth, but she believed too that her sister's mind was, and always had been, affected.

'It was Leslie, I suppose?' she said, but without conviction.

'Leslie, the murderer?' said Miss Trubb. 'Oh, no. Certainly not. The child was destroyed to remove Leslie's power and to remove me. If they had hanged me, there would have been no more blackmail. There was none while I was shut up, was there? The temporary publicity and damage were over. You'd survived it. But when I was released, that was different. That was something new. There'd be a fine new scandal if the facts were known. Perjury, letting me suffer in your place! Respectable, respected citizens, the mother of an illegitimate child! It could be worked up nicely, and I'm sure Leslie did work it up.'

'He did. Oh, he did!' said Frances, bitterly.

'It was because I was afraid of it that I tried to hide from you all when I came out.'

'You might have changed the name,' said Frances. 'Why didn't you go back to your own?'

'I swore I never would, until I could use it without shame,' said Miss Trubb, proudly. 'It would have been deceitful to Mr Philpot, and I had to report to the police. Besides, people had forgotten. So many young ones have never heard of me.'

'Leslie heard of you. Trust him!'

'He never would have if Ray hadn't seen me. It was just

bad luck I picked on a district where he was living. He must have told Leslie.'

'So it all started again. The misery. The fear. Having to get the money without it showing. I couldn't, you know. I kept stalling.'

'You mean you've not paid anything since he started again?'

'Nothing. I tell you, I had to put him off. It was awful. Hiding it all from Colin, too.'

'But Colin knew already,' said Miss Trubb.

'Yes. He knew all the time,' echoed Colin, from the door behind them.

CHAPTER 17

The first thing Mr Philpot did that morning when he reached his office was to ring up Warrington-Reeve. The barrister took the call.

'I've been away from town until a week ago,' Mr Philpot explained. 'That's why I haven't contacted you before. I'd like to give you the result of my researches in Conington. Will you come here, or shall I come to you?'

'I'm tied up at the moment,' Warrington-Reeve told him. 'But I'll be through in half an hour.'

'I'll drop round to you, then. In half an hour.'

The two men met cordially. Mr Philpot wasted no time in coming to the point.

'There was a Helen Trubb engaged at the factory in February 1940. From July of that year onwards there was a Miss Helen Trubb working in the secretarial department of another factory, right up to the time of her arrest. But there was yet another Helen Trubb also working in another war factory in the town from April 1940 until the end of May, when she left on account of advanced pregnancy. I can give the police the dates. As I told Reg, I'm in contact with a number of firms in Conington and know the directors personally. They were interested in my having engaged an ex-murderess, and only too pleased to look up their war-time personnel records.'

'One of them is incomplete,' said the barrister.

'Bombing,' answered Mr Philpot, briefly. 'At the end of that year. Part of the building was burned. Some of the records were lost, not all.'

'It's the same pattern all through, you notice,' said Warrington-Reeve. 'Substitution of Helen for Frances. It seems clear enough. We ought to have seen it at the time. Why didn't we, I wonder?'

He was silent, staring out of the window as he always did when perplexed.

'Pressure of work, I expect,' said Mr Philpot, soothingly. 'The solicitor would be short-handed, I suppose, as they all were.'

'Not a bit of it. Stephen was quite a young man then, medically unfit for any kind of national service. Chest trouble, I think. He had both the senior partners with him, then.'

'Simmonds and Simmonds. *Had*, you say?'

'Yes. The old man retired during the war, I believe. He's dead now. His son retired last year, or the year before.'

'Do you mean to say he never took on any more partners? Or they never did? With this Coke a fairly sick man?'

'Do you know, I've never bothered to find out.'

'Don't you think you should?'

The two men exchanged a glance full of meaning.

'Yes,' said the barrister. 'I see what you mean.'

He made a note on his pad.

'Just one thing more,' said Mr Philpot. 'You'd better know that Miss Trubb is going down to Weyford today to see her sister. She finishes work in my office at twelve. I expect she'll be there this afternoon. I've a notion she knows just about all we do, and possibly a good deal more.'

When he had gone Warrington-Reeve stared out of his window for quite five minutes without moving. Then he turned back to his desk with a violent gesture.

'I'm a fool!' he said, aloud. 'An utter, unmitigated ass! I deserve to be disbarred!'

His clerk looked into the room.

'Did you call me, sir?' he asked.

'Yes. Get me Scotland Yard. And ring up Mrs Holmes on the other line. Give her my compliments and ask her to be ready with her husband to drive down to Weyford with me this afternoon. I shall be at her door at one o'clock, precisely.'

'Where are we going?' Mavis asked.

She was sitting beside Warrington-Reeve in the front passenger seat of the Jaguar, and the miles were humming past at a most exhilarating pace.

'First of all to the late Leslie Coke's house, to see the widow, if she will oblige us.'

'I don't suppose she'll be there,' said Reg, from behind him. 'Didn't Mr Coke say she was always in his wife's pocket, and he wished she wouldn't?'

'Quite correct, Reg. I should have remembered that before. But I'm afraid the years are beginning to tell on me.'

Mavis laughed. He was not driving like an old man, nor did he look like one, in spite of his white hair. Of course dark eyes never did fade like blue or grey ones. But still. . . .

'I wouldn't have said so,' she assured him and was surprised at herself for speaking so familiarly.

'That's very kind and flattering of you, Mavis,' he answered, smiling, but keeping his eyes on the road ahead. 'I only wish it were – God damn it, sir, make up your mind!'

They shot round the car that had wavered in towards the verge and then teethered out into the middle of the road, only to stop dead with a sickening jerk as the Jaguar's horn blared.

'As I was saying,' said Warrington-Reeve, in his deliberate voice, 'we have to find Mrs Leslie first, and persuade her to talk to us. And then, as soon as possible, we have to catch up on Miss Trubb. And I hope to God we're in time.'

'In time for what?'

'If I knew exactly, I wouldn't be in such a hurry.'

With this enigmatic statement the barrister relapsed into silence and did not speak again until he drew up at a house on the southern side of Weyford.

There did not seem to be anyone at home. They rang and knocked for some minutes and then gave it up and went back to the car.

'As you thought, Reg. We'll try the other Coke establishment.'

Here they were more fortunate. Mrs Stephen Coke was at home and Mrs Leslie was with her. The visitors were invited indoors. Mavis thought the house looked shabby compared with the Meadows' establishment.

'I do apologize for disturbing you on a Saturday afternoon,' began Warrington-Reeve, 'especially so soon after your very distressing experience.'

He explained briefly who he was, and introduced Mavis and Reg. The two women bowed their heads. The one in deep mourning got out her handkerchief. The other patted her hand.

'I'm sure you appreciate how important it is to find out all we can about that very misleading map that Reg, here, was sent in Mr Bradley's letter, and that must be connected with the hiding of the Road Closed notice, which no doubt was one of the factors in this terrible deed,' Warrington-Reeve went on. 'I understand you could not tell the police exactly when you posted it, Mrs Leslie?'

She shook her head.

'I tried to remember, but I was too upset. Now I feel muddled all the time.'

'Letter?' said her friend. 'You never told me about a letter.'

'Didn't I? Perhaps I didn't. I wouldn't think it was important. Frances Meadows asked me to put it in the post. I remember popping it in my bag, and I can't remember anything more about it.'

'Which day was this?'

They worked it out between them, at some length and with considerable argument. The others waited, outwardly patient, inwardly fuming at the delay.

'Well, that's the best we can do,' said Mrs Stephen, at last.

Warrington-Reeve summed up.

'Mrs Leslie came here direct from Mrs Meadows's house. She had the letter in her bag and left the bag on the hall table because you were in the kitchen. She helped you by peeling and washing vegetables, and then you both had a cup of tea and she went home. She does not remember actually posting the letter, but next day when she did open her bag in the shops there cannot have been a letter there or she would have sent it and remembered.'

The two women agreed to this. Mrs Leslie looked very grave.

'I've thought about this letter myself,' she said. 'I keep wondering why Colin kept it overnight.'

'Frances was just as bad. They both seem to have been as casual as anything over it,' Mrs Stephen pointed out.

There was an awkward pause.

'You weren't exactly brilliant over it, yourself,' added Mrs Stephen, but her friend was looking at Warrington-Reeve with a pathetic expression on her weak pretty face, and did not seem to have heard her.

The visitors trooped out to the car. As they moved away Mavis exclaimed, sharply, 'Stop! Look! Over there!'

The Jaguar ground to an abrupt halt.

'Where? What's the matter?'

'No. Drive on. He's gone, now.'

'What on earth – '

'Drive on! I'll explain as we go.'

The car moved on, at a slow pace, and Mavis gave them the cause of her agitation.

'There was a man standing behind the bushes near the gate. In a grey overcoat and a squashy hat. He was the man I saw in the gardens at home, when Miss Trubb took Joy away. I'm dead sure it was the same!'

'Did you recognize his face?'

'I didn't see his face, either time. Not properly. The clothes were the same.'

'The same as half the population,' said Reg.

Mavis answered, 'It was being half-hidden, like the first time, I suppose. Perhaps I'm being silly.'

'No,' said Warrington-Reeve. 'I'm sure you're not. You never are. Do you think it was anyone you know?'

'I don't think so. I don't know, I tell you.'

'Could it have been Colin Meadows? You've seen him, haven't you?'

'Well, he was about the right height. Oh, I don't know. Forget it. I'm sorry I got excited.'

Warrington-Reeve reached out a hand and patted her arm.

'You mustn't be. You've probably added another important link to the chain. What's the time?' he asked.

'Half-past two,' said Reg.

The two women gasped, instinctively stretched hands to one another, and drew closer together.

163

'Colin has known from the beginning,' said Miss Trubb, 'or very nearly so. Ray told him. That's true, isn't it, Colin?'

'Perfectly,' said the man near the door. He came slowly into the room, unbuttoning his grey overcoat as he did so, and sat down to light a cigarette, while the two women watched him, silent and terrified.

Frances began to shiver.

'Did he know when he – when he married me?'

'Oh, yes. He knew.'

'Then why? Why not – ' She could not finish.

'Tell her why not, Colin,' said Miss Trubb. 'Tell her about your big mistake.'

He winced at the word and the bitterness in her voice, but continued to smoke, not looking at either of them.

'I see I shall have to tell you myself,' Helen went on, drawing Frances closer still, and putting an arm around her. 'Colin was angry with me for leaving Weyford and for asking him to trust me blindly. He thought you were speaking the truth when you told him I was pregnant. He was very upset. Do you know why?'

'Because he loved you,' whispered Frances, and hid her face on her sister's shoulder.

'Oh, no. Not for that. He never loved me. He never loved either of us. Did you, Colin?'

There was still no response.

'He loved the business and the position he designed to get for himself,' went on Miss Trubb. 'While he thought I was having a baby he turned to you. He would have preferred me, because I was more useful in the business, and knew the ins and outs of it. That was why he was so angry with me, he never even took the trouble to find out if you were speaking the truth. That was his big mistake. Because when you got engaged to him, so soon after you had Tom, Ray told him the truth and told him Leslie was the father of the child.'

'Oh, no!' moaned Frances.

'So you see,' Helen went on, steadily, 'he had to go on with it, and suppress the truth from my father. Otherwise you, and not I, would have been disinherited, and I would have been restored to my place in Father's affections. He would have lost his chance to marry me. At least that was what he thought at the time.'

'You are very sure of my thoughts,' said Colin. 'You always were a self-opinionated fool.'

'So I need never have paid Leslie anything?' Frances said. Her sister looked at her, sadly.

'I begged you to confess to Colin. Didn't I? That was before I even knew the whole horrible story.'

Colin turned to look at her for the first time.

'As a matter of interest,' he said, 'when exactly did you find out? And how?'

'When Leslie came to see me at Sandfields Avenue, after Ray had told him where I was.'

'And after he'd already come to me again for money! I mean Leslie,' cried Frances.

'The bastard was trying to blackmail both of us,' said Colin, with a short laugh. 'Had been, all along. But I never gave him a penny.'

'But that was why you killed Tom,' said Miss Trubb, steadily, 'hoping to kill me as well.'

Colin got up and stretched himself.

'Leslie was in an inventive mood,' he said, 'that evening you tried to gas yourself.'

'How do you know which day he came to see me?' she asked, knowing the answer. 'Or at what time?'

He laughed again.

'Leslie is dead,' he said. 'So is Thorne. And you're barmy. Certifiable now, wouldn't you say, Frances?'

'No,' she answered, through shaking lips.

That startled him. He knew she had always believed in her sister's guilt.

'She never was,' Frances continued. 'I understand now. She thought I'd done it, and she suffered for my sake. And for your happiness. I knew you never loved me. I thought that was on her account, and I was jealous. But I thought you were good, and after Leslie, I thought I was lucky to get you. God forgive me for a fool!'

'You always were,' said Colin, easily. 'Both of you.'

'But I would never have believed you killed Tom. Not until now.'

He made an impatient gesture.

'What makes you believe it now? You're crazy. You know where I was that night the boy died. You know it as well as you know you were here in Weyford yourself. I went to my parents for a couple of nights after I left the Home. You know that.'

'I know you say so. You can't prove it, now. They're both dead.'

That shook him again. Frances was not quite the meek idiot he had taken her for.

'I'll find a way to prove it, if necessary,' he said. 'But it won't be.'

'Are you sure?' said Miss Trubb, who had gone to the window. 'You'll have to be quick about it, then, because they're here.'

'Who?' He had risen from his chair, but he did not seem afraid, only alert and tense.

'May we come in?' said a voice from the doorway.

Warrington-Reeve, Reg and Mavis walked into the room.

'I do apologize,' the former said to Frances, 'for breaking into your house. But the front door was so invitingly open. How d'you do, Miss Trubb.'

'Who the hell are you?' said Colin, moving forward.

Frances was speechless. It was Miss Trubb who introduced the barrister to Colin and then went to Mavis and stood beside her.

'We have just come from Cokes' house,' said Warrington-Reeve. 'We are trying to find out about that misleading map Reg was sent. The police, as I expect you know, are more interested in determining who killed Leslie. I want to know who tried to kill these two young people.'

'I see,' said Colin. He did not seem to resent their presence any longer. 'I must say I consider any – hazards they may have encountered are entirely their own fault. I took the trouble to go to them in person and tell them so. I believe they had other warnings.'

'That was Ray,' said Miss Trubb. She whispered to Mavis, 'He told me he pinned the notice on the pram. He meant it kindly.'

'It was a clumsy plan,' went on Warrington-Reeve, ignoring

these remarks. 'But I have noticed that all this criminal's activities seem to be a mixture of cunning invention and stupid action. This last example follows the pattern. And it depends primarily upon changing the sketch map made by Mr Bradley. You had every opportunity of doing so, Mr Meadows.'

'Oh, yes,' answered Colin, carelessly, 'but so had my wife and others, I believe. Our Inspector Frost has been into it most carefully with me.'

'Just so. You kept the letter from the afternoon you undertook to post it until the following morning. Did you steam it open and put in another map of your own devising?'

Colin looked at him with contempt.

'I did not,' he said. 'Have you come all the way from London with those two young busybodies to ask me a damn fool question like that? Of course the answer is no.'

'Of course. Mrs Meadows, did you see any signs on the letter of its having been opened?'

'No.' She was breathless and strained, but quite sure of herself. In contrast to the scatter-brained little woman he had seen at Stephen Coke's house.

'Why don't you ask the Cokes?' Colin said. 'We can't help you.'

'I have asked their wives. Unfortunately Leslie is no longer available.'

'Stephen is. Why didn't you get him to do this for you? He briefed you in the first place, didn't he?'

'They have always been our family lawyers,' said Miss Trubb, unnecessarily. 'From grandfather's time.'

'Quite.' Warrington-Reeve turned back to Colin. 'Yes. I must ask Coke. I wonder if you can tell me where I am likely to find him. He was not at home.'

'In the ordinary way he'd be playing a round of golf. As I should, myself. He's probably at the Club.'

'That sounds like a contradiction in terms. Is today something out of the ordinary? Why should he be at the Club, and not playing?'

Colin exploded.

'As if you didn't know! Can't you stop kidding? You know

167

as well as I do half a dozen detectives have been up there since early this morning, and they're not through yet.'

'Through what?' cried Frances. Miss Trubb clasped her hands. Her face had gone very white.

'I came home because I couldn't get a game. They're in the locker room. I don't know what they're up to. But we can't touch a thing, neither clothes nor clubs, till they're through. So I came away.'

'Did you see Coke there this morning?'

'No.'

'But you think he's likely to be there now.'

'How do I know, really? Go and find out.'

'Perhaps you'd like to come with me.'

'Certainly not.'

The telephone bell rang, making Mavis start. Frances answered it.

'For you,' she said to Colin.

He listened, grunted agreement, then put back the receiver and turned to Warrington-Reeve. His face had gone as white as Miss Trubb's, but his voice was steady as he spoke.

'I'll change my mind, if that suits you. It was some pompous ass from Scotland Yard on the line. He wants me to go up there at once. What sort of knot have they tied themselves into this time, I wonder?'

The four of them went out silently and climbed into the Jaguar. As it swept out of the drive Miss Trubb opened her arms, and Frances, with a little sob, stumbled back to that long-lost and sorely-missed protection and love.

CHAPTER 18

The Weyford Golf Club was in turmoil. Members, instead of lounging in armchairs, idly relaxing after a game, or else flipping through a magazine while waiting for a late opponent, were standing about in tense groups, talking loudly, angrily, greedily, about the invasion of their premises by the police, and the possible cause of it.

There were older members who recalled earlier scandals, since decently veiled in the past. Depredations by an erring Secretary, the arrest of a bar steward for beating up his wife at home the night before. The younger members were not interested. What intrigued them was the continued presence of Stephen Coke. Was he on the job? Waiting to accuse or defend one of themselves? Or just waiting? He had arrived early that morning, and on finding that he could not have his clubs had gone away again. He was back before three, furious to find he still could not play. At least, he had given a good performance of fury. By now there was a firm rumour that the police search had to do with his cousin's murder. Many of the members thought it was slightly indecent of him to sit there in the corner smoking, and chatting from time to time with the various friends who went up to speak to him. Unless he was on the job.

The idea was that the locker room was being searched for clues. Leslie's locker. Not that Leslie had been seen at the Club much in recent months. He had not paid his sub, they said, though the Secretary refused either to confirm or deny this.

When Warrington-Reeve and his party arrived there was a

sudden hush. Curious eyes were turned in his direction. Who were these people with Colin? Why had he brought them there at such an inauspicious moment? Hadn't he gone home in a towering rage less than an hour before?

The barrister spotted Coke at once, and threaded his way to him, followed by Mavis and Reg.

'I hoped I should find you here,' said Warrington-Reeve.

Coke nodded a brief welcome, clearing his coat and hat from the chair beside him.

'Know what they're up to?' the barrister continued, as he sat down.

'Not exactly. I hoped you would. Mitchell is there with some experts he's brought down, and Frost and Willis, of course. They asked me to hang around.' He lowered his voice to say, 'I see you've got Colin with you.'

'We found him at home,' said Warrington-Reeve, easily. 'I'm not sure he wasn't spying on your house before that. Mavis thought she recognized the overcoat of a man near the gate. Like yours,' he added, looking at the garment Coke had just moved. 'The hat, too.'

The solicitor laughed.

'You say "recognized". When has she seen him before?'

'When the child was kidnapped by Miss Trubb. Don't you remember the incident?'

Coke nodded.

'Stupid of me. Of course I remember. Are we getting somewhere at last? Is that why the cops are in possession? Is she sure she saw him? Grey overcoats – '

'Don't say it,' said Warrington-Reeve. 'I know.'

He beckoned to Reg and Mavis, who, deserted by Colin, were standing together at a tactful distance.

'Come and entertain Mr Coke,' he said. 'I'm going to make a frontal assault on the Yard.'

He was gone before Coke, who had half-risen from his chair, could say anything. As the young people moved forward he subsided, welcoming them with a very artificial smile.

Warrington-Reeve was stopped by a constable at the door of the locker room.

'You can't go in, sir,' he said, firmly.

'Then you must take a message,' the barrister told him, with equal authority. 'Tell Detective-Chief-Superintendent Mitchell that Mr Colin Meadows is here, and that I brought him along from his home.'

He held out his card to the constable, who took it doubtfully.

'There is no secret poison on it,' said Warrington-Reeve. 'No hidden radiation. You take it in, there's a good chap. I'll hold the fort for you here while you do.'

Outraged, but overborne, the constable opened the door a crack, and in a loud breathy whisper said, 'Charlie!'

Through the crack a returning whisper said, 'What is it?'

The card disappeared inside, and presently Charlie opened the door wide and said, 'Come in, sir, please.'

The room, not a large one, was full of busy men, engaged, it seemed, upon a sort of conveyor belt system, whereby golf clubs, golf bags, and clothes were numbered, recorded, examined superficially, examined closely by lens and powder, sorted out, discarded, re-examined, and tested in various ways, before finally being returned, reassembled into groups, checked and put back where they came from.

'Well,' said Warrington-Reeve. 'Well, well, well!'

MItchell came forward.

'Nearly through,' he said. 'And we've got him, I think.'

'Who?'

'The man who killed Leslie Coke.'

'With a golf club, I presume?'

'That's the idea.'

'It occurred to me, too. The blow could be delivered from some distance off; I mean, the length of the handle away, and the weapon could be washed by reaching it down into the river. It could be effectively hidden by simply taking it away in the bag.'

'Exactly. And, as usual, he made one mistake. Fortunately for us.'

One of the white-coated specialists at a small improvised laboratory bench in the corner of the room looked up and said to Mitchell, 'Same blood group. That fixes it, I imagine.'

'We'd better have them in, then,' said Mitchell.

'In the lounge,' said Inspector Frost to Sergeant Willis.

'Charlie,' said Sergeant Willis.

The two men went out and came back almost at once with Colin and Stephen Coke.

'Mr Meadows,' said Superintendent Mitchell, 'did you play golf on the morning of the day Leslie Coke was murdered?'

'Yes.'

'Did you finish your game about twelve noon?'

'Just after.'

'What did you do with your clubs then?'

'Put them in my locker in here, and shut it.'

'Are you sure you did not take them away with you and go down to the river on your motor-bike?'

'I did not.'

'And, leaving it hidden, walk along the bank to where the bridge is down, and wait there, concealed in the trees?'

'Of course not. I went for a ride on the bike. I've told you that already, several times.'

Mitchell stretched out a hand. Inspector Frost handed him a club. It was an iron of a rather old fashioned make, with a steel handle.

'Is this one of your clubs, Mr Meadows? You may take it in your hand to look at it.'

'I don't need to. Yes, it's mine. But I hardly ever use it.'

'You hardly ever use it. Can you remember when you last did so?'

'No. It must be years. I'd almost forgotten I still kept the thing in my bag.'

'Did you not use it on that Sunday morning to break open the skull of Leslie Coke?'

Colin took a step backward, only to find Charlie immediately behind him.

'You must be mad!' he panted, his face very white. 'I did no such thing! I swear I didn't!'

'But there is blood on the handle of that club,' said Mitchell, 'and it belongs to the same group as Leslie Coke's blood.'

Colin choked and swayed. Warrington-Reeve took his arm and helped him to a chair, where he slumped with his head between his knees.

'Mr Coke,' said Mitchell, turning to the solicitor, who was

watching the scene with grave concern, 'do you ever play golf with Mr Meadows?'

'Yes. Quite often.'

'When would be the last time?'

'Just a few days ago. Middle of the week, wasn't it, Colin?' He got no answer.

'Did you notice this club in his bag on that occasion?'

'I can't say I did. But I don't make a habit of registering other people's clubs.'

'So all you can say is that you play with Mr Meadows fairly often?'

'That is so.'

'Now, Mr Coke, did you play golf on that Sunday morning?'

'Yes, I did.'

'At what time did you stop playing?'

'About half-past twelve. Perhaps a little later.'

'Did you see Mr Meadows playing that morning?'

'Yes. I was only two holes ahead of him.'

'But he says he finished at twelve. Did he pass in front of you, then?'

'Yes. I lost a ball. I expect he went through, then.'

'Didn't you see him go through?'

'No, My ball had left the course.'

'How long were you in the Club after you stopped playing?'

'A few minutes.'

'Had you been playing alone?'

'Yes. I often go round alone.'

'Did Mr Meadows come into the locker room while you were putting away your clubs?'

'No, I don't think so. I didn't see him. I don't think he was in the Club House.'

'Did you go home by car?'

'Yes. My wife would probably remember what time I got back.'

'Did that search for your ball take you to the river, Mr Coke? To the place where the bridge is down?'

Colin sat up with a jerk. Warrington-Reeve laid a hand on his shoulder. The solicitor gave a curious little laugh.

'Is this a joke?' he asked.

'No. It is not a joke. Did you go there?'

'Of course not.'

'Did you strike Leslie Coke, your cousin, with the club you had at some time taken from Mr Meadow's bag?'

'What is all this?' cried Coke, loudly and aggressively. 'Warrington-Reeve, have they taken leave of their senses? Colin has practically confessed. Look at him! They've proved he did it. Why don't they charge him? Why ask me these ridiculous questions?'

'They have not taken leave of their senses,' said the barrister. 'I'm afraid you were not quite clever enough, at this stage, or any other.'

Coke drew himself up, his teeth bared in contempt and fury, his thin body quivering. A rat, thought Warrington-Reeve, but a fighting rat. There might be trouble yet.

'I did *not* kill my cousin!' Stephen cried. 'You have already said there was blood on Colin's club.'

'Yes,' answered Mitchell. 'There was a small quantity of dried blood on the handle of his club, but there was no blood at all on the sides or bottom of his golf-bag. That suggests that when the club was returned to the bag, the blood was already dry. But in your bag, Mr Coke, there are small blood stains near and on the bottom. Which suggests that the club was put into *your* bag when the blood was *fresh*. You should have taken more care to wash *both* ends of the club thoroughly. Or did it come from your hands or your shoes, before you wiped them in the grass, looking for the lost ball?'

Coke was still fighting. He could not believe his splendid plan had failed. Deep in his heart the consciousness of ultimate failure sapped his strength. But he still fought.

'So what?' he said, trying to make his voice sound as defiant as he felt. 'Why couldn't he have put that club in my bag as easily as – you say I put it in his?'

They all noticed the way he had tripped. But he persisted.

'Anyway, what motive would I have? Tell me that.'

'The motive we originally thought Mr Meadows had,' said Mitchell. 'Blackmail. Your books and accounts don't lie, Mr Coke.'

He turned and dived for the door. His movement was so quick and, at that moment, so unexpected, except by the barrister, that he had wrenched the door open and was through it before the police were able to move. But the next out was Warrington-Reeve, shouting to Reg, 'Head him off his car, Reg. Coke's our man!'

Reg was astounded, but obeyed without question. He jumped for the door of the lounge, and straddled the corridor just in time. Coke rushed into the lounge, pushed through the bewildered crowd, smashed his way through a window and, dropping on to the turf below, made off up the fairway of the first hole.

His flight was pointless and he knew it. Knew his defeat, its nearness, its completeness, from his weakening muscles, and failing breath. But he could not give in. He must gain the shelter of the trees and have time to think. There must be some way – even now.

The police, momentarily taken off their guard, recovered very quickly. The two constables were big men, slow-moving, but Frost and Willis were younger, more athletic, and determined to make the arrest. They went out through the broken window like prize hurdlers, while the members of the Club, having unbolted the double french windows, poured out to watch the chase, Warrington-Reeve among them.

'Come back!' shouted the barrister, as Reg sprinted off, easily catching up and overtaking the two detectives. 'He's got a knife!'

At this moment two newcomers emerged from the Club House, members who always arrived late, fastidious members, who kept their clubs in their own homes, and repainted their own balls. They passed through the excited crowd and moved towards the first tee. They did not seem to notice the stumbling figure far off nor the three running behind.

In a flash Warrington-Reeve snatched the club from the hand of one, the ball from the other. He cleared a space for himself with a sweep of the arm, placed his ball, swung, and immediately after bellowed, 'Fore!'

The detectives, being countrymen, and conversant with the game, fanned to either side of the course, but continued running. Reg simply ignored the call. But Mr Coke automatically stopped dead, and turned, and received the ball straight on the windpipe, just where the breast bone ends. He gave a gurgling cry and collapsed backwards on to the ground, hearing as he fell a roar of primitive, spontaneous, callous laughter from the massed spectators. Reg found him limp, sobbing, and kicked the knife from his hand. After that he showed fight, struggling and biting, but the young man held him down until the other two arrived to secure him.

At the Club House, shocked by the manner of the arrest and its reception, Superintendent Mitchell explained briefly what had happened. As he went forward to meet the prisoner and charge him, followed by Warrington-Reeve, he heard a member say, 'The way he sat down backwards! That shot really was an absolutely marvellous fluke!' To which the other replied, 'Fluke, my foot! That was Warrington-Reeve, Q.C. Thirty years ago he was mopping up championships all round the country. Didn't know the old boy had kept his hand in so well.'

Miss Trubb was having tea with Mrs Ford. On the hearthrug Joy was alternately crawling and collapsing. Mavis was out.

'You don't know what a relief it is to me that Colin is cleared,' said Miss Trubb. 'Not that he's much good to Frances, but she's still fond of him, and then there are the children. It was silly of me to suspect him. He's much too sharp to do all the silly things Stephen did. I must say I didn't think it was him until Leslie and Raymond were killed on the same day. Even then I still thought Frances had smothered little Tom. To think I needn't have held my tongue, right from the start.'

'It always pays to tell the truth,' said Mrs Ford. 'And to speak out, too.'

'I suppose it does. Colin wouldn't have minded the scandal about Frances or the publicity, once he got his hands on the business.'

'That's just what Reg and Mavis thought of him.' Mrs Ford poured Miss Trubb another cup, then she asked, 'What was Stephen Coke's motive really?'

'Money,' said Miss Trubb, 'at the start. We didn't know it, but he was as bad as Leslie over gambling. He got into debt, and he couldn't pay. It came to a head when Father died, it seems. Knowing Frances was ignorant of the business and Father's will gave her the whole estate, he took enough to clear himself. Then he realized that with Father gone I might not stay hidden away with the baby, and I might ask awkward questions about the money, and perhaps offer to help Frances with managing it. He thought he'd get rid of me, but I think Leslie must have realized his action, and blackmailed him for it. Then with Reg and Mavis getting Mr Reeve interested he got really frightened it would all come out, the embezzling and all, so he killed him, and Ray, too.'

'He really did kill Mr Thorne?'

'They found him guilty of multiple murder, didn't they? He could have. They found he was with Ray that night, late, and he had some barbiturate of the same kind; at least his wife had.'

'The wicked scoundrel!' said Mrs Ford. 'Acting the family lawyer with that on his conscience.'

'No wonder my defence didn't go very deep,' said Miss Trubb, bitterly. 'Mr Reeve did his best, but there was Stephen to hamper him at every turn.'

'They brought out the blackmail at the trial,' said Mrs Ford.

'Yes. That was what put them on to Stephen. Leslie had received money, but neither Frances nor Colin had given it to him. Nor anyone else they could find. They traced it to Stephen. It was Mr Philpot's suggestion, really. He was surprised Stephen's firm had gone to pieces. Only him left. You see, in business, if the partners leave, and the firm contracts, it means either business is falling off, or the partners don't trust the one they leave. It seemed like that to him over Stephen. He was right.'

'Mavis noticed how shabby their house was,' said Mrs Ford. 'She thought they must be helping Mrs Leslie on account of her husband's behaviour.'

'They were. Or Stephen was. That was the way he paid his blackmail. Through Leslie's wife. Scotland Yard traced that. They thought of the golf club, too. They *are* clever.'

'Which Mr Coke was *not*,' said Mrs Ford. 'And his greatest stupidity was in not understanding you, my dear.'

Mavis came in, followed soon after by Reg.

'I've been hearing the inside story of the crime,' said Mrs Ford, complacently. 'If it wasn't true, you'd hardly credit it, would you?'

'There's one or two things I've longed to ask you, Miss Trubb,' began Mavis.

'Helen,' said Miss Trubb.

'Helen. That first gas smell.'

'Oh, that,' she laughed. 'I felt so awful after Leslie went. He hinted at danger, without saying where from. Naturally I thought of Frances. So I went down to get myself a hot drink, and let it boil over.'

'Exactly what we guessed. Aren't we brilliant?'

'The other thing was your note,' said Reg. 'The wavy edge. Who did that?'

'I did that, too. I'd put down where I was going, which was back to Mrs Ogden, if she'd have me, and then I thought I'd better not tell even you two, so I cut the name out and put the note in your brief-case.'

'While we made it easy for Coke to get in by leaving the kitchen window open.'

'He'd have found a way. Like he did at Conington, taking the front door key. He was coming every few days just after Father died, about the will and that. The key was never missed. I suppose he had it copied.'

Miss Trubb rose to go.

'I must be off now,' she said. 'I just wanted to see you two and thank you. This is the very last time you'll see Helen Trubb.'

'Oh, no!' they all exclaimed together, half laughing, half chilled by her manner.

'No of course not. I'll often look you up,' she promised, smiling, and apologized for giving them one last fright.

But she meant what she had said, she told herself that evening, sitting in the new room she had found for herself, far away from South London, and the Philpots, in a new part of the town where she was quite unknown. And never would be known.

For Mr Reeve had told her only that day that her Queen's Pardon, for a crime she had never committed, had just come through. She was free and safe at last, secure in the old relationship with Frances, happy in the prospect of her new job at a children's orphanage.

She filled her teapot from the boiling kettle, drew her chair closer to the fire, settled her reading lamp conveniently, and in the intervals of eating her leisurely little meal she wrote her thanks to Mr Warrington-Reeve, signing her letter with the name she had never allowed to be dishonoured, but by which she would henceforth always be known, Helen Victoria Clements.

Pandora Women Crime Writers

For further information about Pandora Press
books, please write to the Mailing List Dept. at
Pandora Press, 11 New Fetter Lane, London
EC4P 4EE

THE HOURS BEFORE DAWN
by Celia Fremlin

Behind the curtains of Britain's 1950's suburbia,
a harassed mother is at the end of her tether.
Louise Henderson's kids cry, scream and shout
ceaselessly. Her husband whinges and wants
his dinner on the table, his shirts ironed.
But it's not the suburban mediocrity of her life
that horrifies Louise. There's something about
the lodger she has taken in that terrifies her.
Louise knows she's seen this woman before,
but she can't think where.

Pandora Women Crime Writers
May: LC8: 190pp
Paperback: 0–86358–269–9: £3.95

EASY PREY
by Josephine Bell

Well known to aficionados of crime fiction,
Josephine Bell, author of *The Port of London
Murders*, has created another riveting web of
intrigue and death.
When Reg and Mavis Holmes advertise for a
lodger they get the wonderful Miss Trubb who
seems kind and gentle and ready to help with
their young baby. But Reg and Mavis soon
learn that they've entrusted their 6 month old
daughter to the protection of a convicted child
killer . . .

Pandora Women Crime Writers
May: LC8: 254pp
Paperback: 0–86358–271–0: £3.95

SOMETHING SHADY
by Sarah Dreher

Stoner McTavish, lovable amateur detective
embarks on another adventure in the company
of her girlfriend, Gwen.
A woman has disappeared from her workplace,
a huge shabby country house turned mental
hospital known as Shady Acres. Desperate to
find out what has happened to the woman,
Stoner poses as a mental patient at Shady
Acres . . . with terrifying results.
This is the second in the Stoner McTavish series
by American author Sarah Dreher.

Pandora Women Crime Writers
May: LC8: 264pp
Paperback: 0–86358–241–9: £3.95

MISCHIEF
by Charlotte Armstrong

Made into the film *Don't Bother to Knock*,
starring Marilyn Monroe, this Charlotte
Armstrong novel is a brilliant portrayal of one
tense night in a New York hotel room.
When newspaper editor Peter O. Jones and his
wife Ruth are staying in New York for a night
out they seem quite happy to leave their little
daughter alone with her babysitter in their
plush hotel room.
But for their child it's the start of a night never
to be forgotten, a night that could scar a child
for life, if that life is allowed to continue.

Pandora Women Crime Writers
May: LC8: 190pp
Paperback: 0–86358–272–9

LONDON PARTICULAR
by Christianna Brand

A car crawls through fog-bound London. Its
passengers, a middle-aged doctor and his
anxious female friend, are responding to a call
from a dying man. But this man was not dying
from any sort of illness, it seems more like
murder!
Christianna Brand, author of *Green For Danger*,
has produced another brilliant atmospheric
tale set in a smog-bound London.

Pandora Women Crime Writers
May: LC8: 254pp
Paperback: 0–86358–273–7: £3.95